ADVENTURES ON THE GO

ADVENTURES ON THE GO

ADVENTURES ON THE GO

WINTER, 2021

VOLUME 1 **BOOK 2**

COPYRIGHT© 2021, OFFBEAT PUBLISHING

ISBN: 978-1-950464-07-4 (PAPERBACK)

ISBN: 978-1-950464-06-7 (EBOOK)

letters to the editor:

OffBeatReads@pm.me

Put *Letter to Editor* in Subject. Email content could be published in future *Adventures on the Go*.

WWW.OFFBEATREADS.COM

Editor's Note

T HE OFFBEAT PUBLISHING Team wishes to thank readers of our premier issue released in the fall. Now that *Adventures on the Go* is officially rolling, we're already stepping things up. Beginning with this winter issue, we have a new promise to you:

MORE STORIES, MORE VARIETY.

In his 1785 poem, "The Task", William Cowper first used the phrase, "Variety is the very spice of life...". This statement has since been used and applied in many ways. In the OffBeat offices, our team oftentimes applies it to this *Adventures Project*—book two of which you are holding now. With very few limitations we seek to include a variety, a *cornucopia*, of genres. Within this smattering you'll notice we seek to deliver old classics, old forgotten to seldom-known and new original stories as part of the spice selection. For the most part, consistent readers don't confine themselves to one genre, so we hope you find this an appealing trait, and willingly delve into each issue with curious excitement. You just may find a surprise or hidden treasure.

Remember that letters to the editor, comments *and* questions, are accepted. Put "Letter to the Editor" in the subject, and send to: OFFBEATREADS@PM.ME. Include your legal name. All letters are subject to printing in future issues.

Serious history buffs may want to stand up and point out that Gustave Whitehead may have actually been the first in flight, however, let us save that debate for another day.

While reading Amelia Earhart's autobiography, "The Fun Of It", I stumbled onto an interesting bit of knowledge. We all know of Orville and Wilbur Wright, right? Did you also know their sister Katharine

Wright supported their inventive efforts? Not only did she work at the bicycle shop as the aspirations of flying took her brothers away from business, but she turned money over to them she had earned from teaching Latin and Greek. And that first heavier-than-air plane? Not only did Katharine help pay for it—she worked on building it. In countless ways Katharine contributed to flight. Thankfully, the brothers frequently gave her credit. I quote Orville from one occasion: "When the world speaks of the Wrights, it must include our sister. Much of our effort has been inspired by her."

Katherine in Pau, watching Wilbur fly. (Photo used by permission; Courtesy of Special Collections and Archives, Wright State University)

THE WESTERN UNION TELEGRAPH COMPANY,
INCORPORATED
23,000 OFFICES IN AMERICA.   CABLE SERVICE TO ALL THE WORLD.

ROBERT C. CLOWRY, President and General Manager.

RECEIVED at

176 C KA 41 44 Paid,   Via Norfolk Va

Kitty Hawk N C Dec 17

Bishop M Wright

        7 Hawthorne St

Success four flights thursday morning all against twenty one mile wind started from Level with engine power alone average speed through air thirty one miles longest 57 seconds inform Press home Christmas .   Orevelle Wright   525P

Of interest, a telegraph Orville Wright sent from Kitty Hawk to his father after successful flights.

Just recently, an Associated Press News article (September 22, 2021), explains that there are plans to demolish the first Wright Brothers bicycle shop in Dayton, Ohio. After failing inspections, it was determined the building, "has deteriorated to a point where it can no longer be maintained and redeveloped." Sad.

In this issue we have: Francis Stevens, who definitely broke out in the genres of fantasy and science fiction; The Vampyre, written in 1819 by English physician and writer John William Polidori; A fitting tale for the season by A.M. Barrage; A true account of a High School haunt by Rachel Daugherty (with sources in back); Two original, brand new stories by Michael Brian and Darryle Purcell; and finally, we're grateful to have a three question interview with Joni M. Fisher, author of the Compass Crimes novels.

Perhaps you knew of the historical bit regarding Katherine Wright, perhaps not. As I peruse and research, I frequently discover interesting and even amazing happenings involving real people. I find myself wondering what fascinating truths lay out there, waiting desperately to be rediscovered and not vanish with the passing of time. As if obscure moments had a breath, a pulse—a soul—they wait. As each day's book comes to a close, a shovelful of dirt is tossed upon the forgotten and dismissed. Perhaps we can give the moment a drink and see it and feel it, appreciate its existence—and keep it alive a little longer.

May the stories that once lived always live,

ROBERT KIMBRELL

Corsets to suit your purpose:
waist training, weddings, costumes,
back pain relief, or just for fun.

Orchard Corset

OrchardCorset.com
Ph. 1-866-456-7411

04/23/19
Customer service and sizing experts
Customer service and sizing experts are very helpful and responsive. Feeling great about my order!
koma876omen

04/25/19
Very comfortable
Fits like a glove and is super comfortable. Highly recommend for daily use.
Dayna L.

04/24/19
Gorgeous!
I knew I had to get this one when I saw the teaser picture for it. It's even more gorgeous in person. Fits well even though I have...
Read More
Amy H.

-Sizing Experts Available 7 Days a Week
-Only Steel-Boned Corsets, Never Plastic
-Interest Free Pay Over Time Option!
-Rewards program
-Men's Corsets too

GUEST INTRODUCTION: MICHAEL BRIAN

I F YOU'VE NEVER read anything by Francis Stevens, consider yourself in for a treat. "Friend Island" is a strange, wonderful story, and it's only the tip of the iceberg. Stevens wasn't as prolific as, say, Isaac Asimov, but she wrote five novels and a number of shorter tales, and each occupies a key place in the history of science fiction/fantasy.

The accolades are many: She has been called the, "greatest woman writer of science fiction in the period between Mary Wollstonecraft Shelley and C.L. Moore" ("Partners in Wonder: Women and the Birth of Science Fiction, 1926-1965") and "the woman who invented dark fantasy" ("The Nightmare and Other Tales of Dark Fantasy"). And none other than H.P. Lovecraft himself purportedly was a fan.

Many readers are no doubt wondering right about now, "So why haven't I heard of her?" Good question. But we can all have a hand in rectifying that and placing her on the pedestal where she belongs, next to early sci-fi/fantasy greats such as Jules Verne and H. G. Wells, and alongside her contemporary Edgar Rice Burroughs (the creator of Tarzan and John Carter, among others).

Stevens, the pen name of Gertrude Barrows Bennett (1884-1948), was born in Minneapolis, Minnesota, and was a stenographer for most of her adult life. She turned to writing sci-fi/fantasy to make money, and in the process, she penned one of the first dystopian novels, "The Heads of Cerberus," and cemented her place as a pioneer in the field.

"Friend Island" is a good example of her inventiveness. Set in a time when women have taken their place as the ruling sex. "In what field is not woman our subtle superior?" asks a male character in the story. It's a clever take on the "stranded on a deserted island" trope.

Whether you approach Stevens' work as a fan of early twentieth-century feminist fiction or as a sci-fi/fantasy fan, you'll enjoy this quirky tale. Because above all else, it's simply a good yarn.

FRIEND ISLAND

BY FRANCIS STEVENS

I T WAS UPON the waterfront that I first met her, in one of the shabby little tea shops frequented by able sailoresses of the poorer type. The uptown, glittering resorts of the Lady Aviators' Union were not for such as she.

Stern of feature, bronzed by wind and sun, her age could only be guessed, but I surmised at once that in her I beheld a survivor of the age of turbines and oil engines—a true sea-woman of that elder time when woman's superiority to man had not been so long recognized. When, to emphasize their victory, women in all ranks were sterner than today's need demands.

The spruce, smiling young maidens—engine-women and stokers of the great aluminum rollers, but despite their profession, very neat in gold-braided blue knickers and boleros—these looked askance at the hard-faced relic of a harsher day, as they passed in and out of the shop.

I, however, brazenly ignoring similar glances at myself, a mere male intruding on the haunts of the world's ruling sex, drew a chair up beside the veteran. I ordered a full pot of tea, two cups and a plate of macaroons, and put on my most ingratiating air. Possibly my unconcealed admiration and interest were wiles not exercised in vain. Or the macaroons and tea, both excellent, may have loosened the old sea-woman's tongue. At any rate, under cautious questioning, she had soon launched upon a series of reminiscences well beyond my hopes for color and variety.

"When I was a lass," quoth the sea-woman, after a time, "there was none of this high-flying, gilt-edged, leather-stocking luxury about the sea. We sailed by the power of our oil and gasoline. If they failed on us, like as not 'twas the rubber ring and the rolling wave for ours."

She referred to the archaic practice of placing a pneumatic affair called a life-preserver beneath the arms, in case of that dreaded disaster, now so unheard of, shipwreck.

"In them days there was still many a man bold enough to join our crews. And I've knowed cases," she added condescendingly, "where just by the muscle and brawn of such men some poor sailor lass has reached shore alive that would have fed the sharks without 'em. Oh, I ain't so down on men as you might think. It's the spoiling of them that I don't hold with. There's too much preached nowadays that man is fit for nothing but to fetch and carry and do nurse-work in big child-homes. To my mind, a man who hasn't the nerve of a woman ain't fitted to father children, let alone raise 'em. But that's not here nor there. My time's past, and I know it, or I wouldn't be setting here gossipin' to you, my lad, over an empty teapot."

I took the hint, and with our cups replenished, she bit thoughtfully into her fourteenth macaroon and continued.

"There's one voyage I'm not likely to forget, though I live to be as old as Cap'n Mary Barnacle, of the *Shouter*. 'Twas aboard the old *Shouter* that this here voyage occurred, and it was her last and likewise Cap'n Mary's. Cap'n Mary, she was then that decrepit, it seemed a mercy that she should go to her rest, and in good salt water at that.

"I remember the voyage for Cap'n Mary's sake, but most I remember it because 'twas then that I come the nighest in my life to committin' matrimony. For a man, the man had nerve; he was nearer bein' companionable than any other man I ever seed; and if it hadn't been for just one little event that showed up the—the *mannishness* of him, in a way I couldn't abide, I reckon he'd be keepin' house for me this minute."

"We cleared from Frisco with a cargo of silkateen petticoats for Brisbane. Cap'n Mary was always strong on petticoats. Leather breeches or even half-skirts would ha' paid far better, they being more in demand like, but Cap'n Mary was three-quarters owner, and says she, land women should buy petticoats, and if they didn't it wouldn't be the Lord's fault nor hers for not providing 'em.

"We cleared on a fine day, which is an all sign—or was, then when the weather and the seas o' God still counted in the trafficking of the humankind. Not two days out we met a whirling, mucking bouncer of a gale that well nigh threw the old *Shouter* a full point off her course in the first wallop. She was a stout craft, though. None of your featherweight, gas-lightened, paper-thin alloy shells, but toughened aluminum from stern to stern. Her turbine drove her through the combers at a forty-five knot clip, which named her a speedy craft for a freighter in them days.

"But this night, as we tore along through the creaming green billows, something unknown went 'way wrong down below.

"I was forward under the shelter of her long over-sloop, looking for a hairpin I'd dropped somewheres about that afternoon. It was a gold hairpin, and gold still being mighty scarce when I was a girl, a course I valued it. But suddenly I felt the old *Shouter* give a jump under my feet like a plane struck by a shell in full flight. Then she trembled all over for a full second, frightened like. Then, with the crash of doomsday ringing in my ears, I felt myself sailing through the air right into the teeth o' the shrieking gale, as near as I could judge. Down I come in the hollow of a monstrous big wave, and as my ears doused under I thought I heard a splash close by. Coming up, sure enough, there close by me was floating a new, patent, hermetic, thermo-ice-chest. Being as it was empty, and being as it was shut up air-tight, that ice-chest made as sweet a life-preserver as a woman could wish in such an hour. About ten foot by twelve, it floated high in the raging sea. Out on its top I scrambled, and hanging on by a handle I looked expectant for some of my poor fellow-women to come floating by. Which they never did, for the good reason that the *Shouter* had blowed up and went below, petticoats, Cap'n Mary and all."

"What caused the explosion?" I inquired.

"The Lord and Cap'n Mary Barnacle can explain," she answered piously. "Besides the oil for her turbines, she carried a power of gasoline for her alternative engines, and likely 'twas the cause of her ending so sudden like. Anyways, all I ever seen of her again was the empty ice-chest that Providence had well-nigh hove upon my head. On that I sat and floated, and floated and sat some more, till by-and-by the storm sort of blowed itself out, the sun come shining—this was next morning—and I could dry my hair and look about me. I was a young lass, then, and not bad to look upon. I didn't want to die, any more than you that's sitting there this minute. So I up and prays for land. Sure enough toward evening a speck heaves up low down on the horizon. At first I took it for a gas liner, but later found it was just a little island, all alone by itself in the great Pacific Ocean.

"Come, now, here's luck, thinks I, and with that I deserts the ice-chest, which being empty, and me having no ice to put in it, not likely to have in them latitudes, is of no further use to me. Striking out I swum a mile or so and set foot on dry land for the first time in nigh three days.

"Pretty land it were, too, though bare of human life as an iceberg in the Arctic.

"I had landed on a shining white beach that run up to a grove of lovely, waving palm trees. Above them I could see the slopes of a hill so high and green it reminded me of my own old home, up near Couquomgo-moc Lake in Maine. The whole place just seemed to smile and smile at me. The palms waved and bowed in the sweet breeze, like they wanted to say, 'Just set right down and make yourself to home. We've been waiting a long time for you to come.' I cried, I was that happy to be made welcome. I was a young lass then, and sensitive-like to how folks treated me. You're laughing now, but wait and see if or not there was sense to the way I felt.

"So I up and dries my clothes and my long, soft hair again, which was well worth drying, for I had far more of it than now. After that I walked along a piece, until there was a sweet little path meandering away into the wild woods.

"Here, thinks I, this looks like inhabitants. Be they civil or wild, I wonder? But after traveling the path a piece, lo and behold it ended sudden like in a wide circle of green grass, with a little spring of clear water. And the first thing I noticed was a slab of white board nailed to a palm tree close to the spring. Right off I took a long drink, for you better believe I was thirsty, and then I went to look at this board. It had evidently been tore off the side of a wooden packing box, and the letters was roughly printed in lead pencil.

"'Heaven help whoever you be,' I read. 'This island ain't just right. I'm going to swim for it. You better too. Good-by. Nelson Smith.' That's what it said, but the spellin' was simply awful. It all looked quite new and recent, as if Nelson Smith hadn't more than a few hours before he wrote and nailed it there.

"Well, after reading that queer warning I begun to shake all over like in a chill. Yes, I shook like I had the ague, though the hot tropic sun was burning down right on me and that alarming board. What had scared Nelson Smith so much that he had swum to get away? I looked all around real cautious and careful, but not a single frightening thing could I behold. And the palms and the green grass and the flowers still smiled that peaceful and friendly like. 'Just make yourself to home,' was wrote all over the place in plainer letters than those sprawly lead pencil ones on the board.

"Pretty soon, what with the quiet and all, the chill left me. Then I thought, 'Well, to be sure, this Smith person was just an ordinary man, I reckon, and likely he got nervous of being so alone. Likely he just fancied things which was really not. It's a pity he drowned himself before I come, though likely I'd have found him poor company. By his record I judge him a man of but common education.'

"So I decided to make the most of my welcome, and that I did for weeks to come. Right near the spring was a cave, dry as a biscuit box, with a nice floor of white sand. Nelson had lived there too, for there was a litter of stuff—tin cans—empty—scraps of newspapers and the like. I got to calling him Nelson in my mind, and then Nelly, and wondering if he was dark or fair, and how he come to be cast away there all alone, and what was the strange events that drove him to his end. I cleaned out the cave, though. He had devoured all his tin-canned provisions, however he come by them, but this I didn't mind. That there island was a generous body. Green milk-coconuts, sweet berries, turtle eggs and the like was my daily fare.

"For about three weeks the sun shone every day, the birds sang and the monkeys chattered. We was all one big, happy family, and the more I explored that island the better I liked the company I was keeping. The land was about ten miles from beach to beach, and never a foot of it that wasn't sweet and clean as a private park.

"From the top of the hill I could see the ocean, miles and miles of blue water, with never a sign of a gas liner, or even a little government running-boat. Them running-boats used to go most everywhere to keep the seaways clean of derelicts and the like. But I knowed that if this island was no more than a hundred miles off the regular courses of navigation, it might be many a long day before I'd be rescued. The top of the hill, as I found when first I climbed up there, was a wore-out crater. So I knowed that the island was one of them volcanic ones you run across so many of in the seas between Capricorn and Cancer.

"Here and there on the slopes and down through the jungly tree-growth, I would come on great lumps of rock, and these must have came up out of that crater long ago. If there was lava it was so old it had been covered up entire with green growing stuff. You couldn't have found it without a spade, which I didn't have nor want."

"Well, at first I was happy as the hours was long. I wandered and clambered and waded and swum, and combed my long hair on the beach, having fortunately not lost my side-combs nor the rest of my gold hairpins. But by-and-by it begun to get just a bit lonesome. Funny thing, that's a feeling that, once it starts, it gets worse and worser so quick it's perfectly surprising. And right then was when the days begun to get gloomy. We had a long, sickly hot spell, like I never seen before on an ocean island. There was dull clouds across the sun from morn to night. Even the little monkeys and parrakeets, that had seemed so gay, moped and drowsed like they was sick. All one day I cried, and let the rain soak me through and through—that was the first rain we had—and I didn't get thorough dried even during the night, though I slept in my cave. Next morning I got up mad as thunder at myself and all the world.

"When I looked out the black clouds was billowing across the sky. I could hear nothing but great breakers roaring in on the beaches, and the wild wind raving through the lashing palms.

"As I stood there a nasty little wet monkey dropped from a branch almost on my head. I grabbed a pebble and slung it at him real vicious. 'Get away, you dirty little brute!' I shrieks, and with that there come a awful blinding flare of light. There was a long, crackling noise like a bunch of Chinese fireworks, and then a sound as if a whole fleet of *Shouters* had all went up together.

"When I come to, I found myself 'way in the back of my cave, trying to dig further into the rock with my finger nails. Upon taking thought, it come to me that what had occurred was just a lightning-clap, and going to look, sure enough there lay a big palm tree right across the glade. It was all busted and split open by the lightning, and the little monkey was under it, for I could see his tail and his hind legs sticking out.

"Now, when I set eyes on that poor, crushed little beast I'd been so mean to, I was terrible ashamed. I sat down on the smashed tree and considered and considered. How thankful I had ought to have been. Here I had a lovely, plenteous island, with food and water to my taste, when it might have been a barren, starvation rock that was my lot. And so, thinking, a sort of gradual peaceful feeling stole over me. I got cheerfuller and cheerfuller, till I could have sang and danced for joy.

"Pretty soon I realized that the sun was shining bright for the first time that week. The wind had stopped hollering, and the waves had died to just a singing murmur on the beach. It seemed kind o' strange, this sudden peace, like the cheer in my own heart after its rage and storm. I rose up, feeling sort of queer, and went to look if the little monkey had came alive again, though that was a fool thing, seeing he was laying all crushed up and very dead. I buried him under a tree root, and as I did it a conviction come to me.

"I didn't hardly question that conviction at all. Somehow, living there alone so long, perhaps my natural womanly intuition was stronger than ever before or since, and so I *knowed*. Then I went and pulled poor Nelson Smith's board off from the tree and tossed it away for the tide to carry off. That there board was an insult to my island!"

The sea-woman paused, and her eyes had a far-away look. It seemed as if I and perhaps even the macaroons and tea were quite forgotten.

"Why did you think that?" I asked, to bring her back. "How could an island be insulted?"

She started, passed her hand across her eyes, and hastily poured another cup of tea.

"Because," she said at last, poising a macaroon in mid-air, "because that island—that particular island that I had landed on—had a heart!

"When I was gay, it was bright and cheerful. It was glad when I come, and it treated me right until I got that grouchy it had to mope from sympathy. It loved me like a friend. When I flung a rock at that poor little drenched monkey critter, it backed up my act with an anger like the wrath o' God, and killed its own child to please me! But it got right cheery the minute I seen the wrongness of my ways. Nelson Smith had no business to say, 'This island ain't just right,' for it was a righter place than ever I seen elsewhere. When I cast away that lying board, all the birds begun to sing like mad. The green milk-coconuts fell right and left. Only the monkeys seemed kind o' sad like still, and no wonder. You see, their own mother, the island, had rounded on one o' them for my sake!

"After that I was right careful and considerate. I named the island Anita, not knowing her right name, or if she had any. Anita was a pretty name, and it sounded kind of South Sea like. Anita and me got along real well together from that day on. It was some strain to be always gay and singing around like a dear duck of a canary bird, but I done my best. Still, for all the love and gratitude I bore Anita, the company of an island, however sympathetic, ain't quite enough for a human being. I still got lonesome, and there was even days when I couldn't keep the clouds clear out of the sky, though I will say we had no more tornadoes.

"I think the island understood and tried to help me with all the bounty and good cheer the poor thing possessed. None the less my heart give a wonderful big leap when one day I seen a blot on the horizon. It drawed nearer and nearer, until at last I could make out its nature."

"A ship, of course," said I, "and were you rescued?"

"'Tweren't a ship, neither," denied the sea-woman somewhat impatiently. "Can't you let me spin this yarn without no more remarks and fool questions? This thing what was bearing down so fast with the incoming tide was neither more nor less than another island!

"You may well look startled. I was startled myself. Much more so than you, likely. I didn't know then what you, with your book-learning, very likely know now—that islands sometimes float. Their underparts being a tangled-up mess of roots and old vines that new stuff's growed over, they sometimes break away from the mainland in a brisk gale and go off for a voyage, calm as a old-fashioned, eight-funnel steamer. This one was uncommon large, being as much as two miles, maybe, from shore to shore. It had its palm trees and its live things, just like my own Anita, and I've sometimes wondered if this drifting piece hadn't really been a part of my island once—just its daughter like, as you might say.

"Be that, however, as it might be, no sooner did the floating piece get within hailing distance than I hears a human holler and there was a man dancing up and down on the shore like he was plumb crazy. Next minute he had plunged into the narrow strip of water between us and in a few minutes had swum to where I stood.

"Yes, of course it was none other than Nelson Smith!

"I knowed that the minute I set eyes on him. He had the very look of not having no better sense than the man what wrote that board and then nearly committed suicide trying to get away from the best island in all the oceans. Glad enough he was to get back, though, for the coconuts was running very short on the floater what had rescued him, and the turtle eggs wasn't worth mentioning. Being short of grub is the surest way I know to cure a man's fear of the unknown."

"Well, to make a long story short, Nelson Smith told me he was a aeronauter. In them days to be an aeronauter was not the same as to be an aviatress is now. There was dangers in the air, and dangers in the sea, and he had met with both. His gas tank had leaked and he had dropped into the water close by Anita. A case or two of provisions was all he could save from the total wreck.

"Now, as you might guess, I was crazy enough to find out what had scared this Nelson Smith into trying to swim the Pacific. He told me a story that seemed to fit pretty well with mine, only when it come to the scary part he shut up like a clam, that aggravating way some men have. I give it up at last for just man-foolishness, and we begun to scheme to get away.

"Anita moped some while we talked it over. I realized how she must be feeling, so I explained to her that it was right needful for us to get with our kind again. If we stayed with her we should probably quarrel like cats, and maybe even kill each other out of pure human cussedness. She cheered up considerable after that, and even, I thought, got a little anxious to have us leave. At any rate, when we begun to provision up the little floater, which we had anchored to the big island by a cable of twisted bark, the green nuts fell all over the ground, and Nelson found more turtle nests in a day than I had in weeks.

"During them days I really got fond of Nelson Smith. He was a companionable body, and brave, or he wouldn't have been a professional aeronauter, a job that was rightly thought tough enough for a woman, let alone a man. Though he was not so well educated as me, at least he was quiet and modest about what he did know, not like some men, boasting most where there is least to brag of.

"Indeed, I misdoubt if Nelson and me would not have quit the sea and the air together and set up housekeeping in some quiet little town up in New England, maybe, after we had got away, if it had not been for what happened when we went. I never, let me say, was so deceived in any man before nor since. The thing taught me a lesson and I never was fooled again.

"We was all ready to go, and then one morning, like a parting gift from Anita, come a soft and favoring wind. Nelson and I run down the beach together, for we didn't want our floater to blow off and leave us. As we was running, our arms full of coconuts, Nelson Smith, stubbed his bare toe on a sharp rock, and down he went. I hadn't noticed, and was going on.

"But sudden the ground begun to shake under my feet, and the air was full of a queer, grinding, groaning sound, like the very earth was in pain.

"I turned around sharp. There sat Nelson, holding his bleeding toe in both fists and giving vent to such awful words as no decent sea-going lady would ever speak nor hear to!

"'Stop it, stop it!' I shrieked at him, but 'twas too late.

"Island or no island, Anita was a lady, too! She had a gentle heart, but she knowed how to behave when she was insulted.

"With one terrible, great roar a spout of smoke and flame belched up out o' the heart of Anita's crater hill a full mile into the air!

"I guess Nelson stopped swearing. He couldn't have heard himself, anyways. Anita was talking now with tongues of flame and such roars as would have bespoke the raging protest of a continent.

"I grabbed that fool man by the hand and run him down to the water. We had to swim good and hard to catch up with our only hope, the floater. No bark rope could hold her against the stiff breeze that was now blowing, and she had broke her cable. By the time we scrambled aboard great rocks was falling right and left. We couldn't see each other for a while for the clouds of fine gray ash.

"It seemed like Anita was that mad she was flinging stones after us, and truly I believe that such was her intention. I didn't blame her, neither!

"Lucky for us the wind was strong and we was soon out of range.

"'So!' says I to Nelson, after I'd got most of the ashes out of my mouth, and shook my hair clear of cinders. 'So, that was the reason you up and left sudden when you was there before! You aggravated that island till the poor thing druv you out!'

"'Well,' says he, and not so meek as I'd have admired to see him, 'how could I know the darn island was a lady?'

"'Actions speak louder than words,' says I. 'You should have knowed it by her ladylike behavior!'

"'Is volcanoes and slingin' hot rocks ladylike?'he says. 'Is snakes ladylike? T'other time I cut my thumb on a tin can, I cussed a little bit. Say— just a li'l' bit! An' what comes at me out o' all the caves, and out o' every crack in the rocks, and out o' the very spring o' water where I'd been drinkin'? Why snakes! *Snakes*, if you please, big, little, green, red and sky-blue-scarlet! What'd I do? Jumped in the water, of course. Why wouldn't I? I'd ruther swim and drown than be stung or swallowed to death. But how was I t' know the snakes come outta the rocks because I cussed?'

"'You, couldn't,' I agrees, sarcastic. 'Some folks never knows a lady till she up and whangs 'em over the head with a brick. A real, gentle, kind-like warning, them snakes were, which you would not heed! Take shame to yourself, Nelly,' says I, right stern, 'that a decent little island like Anita can't associate with you peaceable, but you must hurt her sacredest feelings with language no lady would stand by to hear!'

"I never did see Anita again. She may have blew herself right out of the ocean in her just wrath at the vulgar, disgustin' language of Nelson Smith. I don't know. We was took off the floater at last, and I lost track of Nelson just as quick as I could when we was landed at Frisco.

"He had taught me a lesson. A man is just full of mannishness, and the best of 'em ain't good enough for a lady to sacrifice her sensibilities to put up with.

"Nelson Smith, he seemed to feel real bad when he learned I was not for him, and then he apologized. But apologies weren't no use to me. I could never abide him, after the way he went and talked right in the presence of me and my poor, sweet lady friend, Anita!"

Now I am well versed in the lore of the sea in all ages. Through mists of time I have enviously eyed wild voyagings of sea rovers who roved and spun their yarns before the stronger sex came into its own, and ousted man from his heroic pedestal. I have followed—across the printed page—the wanderings of Odysseus. Before Gulliver I have burned the incense of tranced attention; and with reverent awe considered the history of one Munchausen, a baron. But alas, these were only men!

In what field is not woman our subtle superior?

Meekly I bowed my head, and when my eyes dared lift again, the ancient mariness had departed, leaving me to sorrow for my surpassed and outdone idols. Also with a bill for macaroons and tea of such incredible proportions that in comparison therewith I found it easy to believe her story!

MOMENT IN HISTORY

Billie Holiday, February 1947 at Downbeat,
a New York jazz club.

THE GOOD GUY

BY DARRYLE PURCELL

IT WAS HIGH noon and I was worn out after a two-week ride from Tucson to Corriganville, Arizona. As we rode into town, my gut churned with a combination of dread and the lingering effects of Whiny's adobe biscuits and buffalo swamp gravy. I don't know who told that grizzled old sidewinder he could cook, but I'd bet my silver-studded saddle the man is dead.

I'm Buck West. At that time, I was a travelin' cowpoke from somewhere on the good side of the Panhandle. And I was worn out. My black hair stayed unruffled thanks to dried sweat and trail dust, while keeping my large white sombrero stuck on my head. Thanks to that same material my light gray cayuse, Arrow, had kicked up during the whole trip, my formerly white bandana and gray cavalry shirt matched perfectly. I really needed a bath.

My sidekick, Whiny, always caused a stir when we came into a new town, as the noise from his horseless contraption scared everyone and everything within hearing, causing horses to yank themselves free from hitching posts and run, women to drop their bags of doodads and whatchamacallits, shop owners to lock their doors and wandering dogs to wet themselves.

The loud popping, grumbling, roaring, rusty-iron wagon was about the size of a child's goat cart. Whiny would pour a jug of firewater into a tank, crank a metal handle in the front of the thing and it would commence to bounce and rumble, hauling that old coot and whatever he had piled behind the seat wherever he wanted to go.

That unsuccessful bearded old prospector would never tell me where he got the thing, or even why he wanted to keep it. It always embarrassed the heck out of me whenever anyone saw us together. Even Delores, Whiny's Burro, hated the contraption. Unfortunately for her, she was tied to the back of it and had to keep pace. I always figured, sooner or later she would turn around and kick that hell-spawn frying pan on wheels into the next territory.

"Get that overbuilt butter churn off the streets!" a big man wearing a star on his leather vest hollered.

Whiny turned the contraption into an alley and, with the flick of a switch, caused the thing to pop louder than a shotgun, blowing black smoke into the air and bringing about a complete silence to the area.

"What the heck is that thing?" the sheriff yelled.

"You don't hafta holler," Whiny lectured. "I ain't deef!"

I turned to the lawman and explained, "He doesn't know. It's just some device that he came upon while prospecting in some gawdawful wasteland."

I felt like an idiot trying to explain Whiny's Model X to the lawman. The only thing I really knew about it was that Whiny was controlling it when I first met him, just after the war. I had wondered at that time, what the grizzled reb, who was older than soot in '65, was doing with the thing. And, if someone in the Confederacy could have built such a machine, how is it that we lost?

That was 20 years prior to our visit to Corriganville, and Whiny still looked the same—like he might have once been a personal friend of Christopher Columbus. Come to think of it, I hadn't change a bit during that time either—still over six feet tall, strong jawed and handsome, according to several young ladies whom I had helped during those two decades.

That's where my feelings of dread came in. Whiny and I had ridden into hundreds of towns that looked exactly like Corriganville (in fact, the streets and buildings were identical except for the business signage). And every time, we seemed to get conscripted into helping young ladies keep their ranches, protecting schoolmarms from lecherous saloon owners, rescuing herds from phantom rustlers and, basically, tracking down a few no-good blackguards and bringing them to justice.

And, usually, my reward for such heroic actions would be a kiss from an appreciative, pretty lady. You'd think I'd be happy. But I had begun to wonder why I would always jump on my horse and ride away right after that one short snuggle. Something just didn't seem right.

Oh, I understand that quite often duty called and I didn't have time to linger. Another odd circumstance was that something always seemed to happen about that same moment I would be trying to press lips with an appreciative filly. Whiny would fall out of tree, Delores would shove the old man into a pond or a dog would just bark and everyone would laugh. Coincidence? I was beginning to wonder.

As the sheriff joined a few cowpokes, ladies, children and dogs to inspect the horseless machine, Whiny jumped up onto the boarded walkway and started slapping his beat-up old chapeau against his clothes, causing a gargantuan dust cloud.

"Dag-flap it!" he sputtered. "I got enough soil on my tongue to plant an acre of corn. Let's meander into that saloon so I could pour some liquor on my licker. Hee-hya!"

I used both hands to push the swinging doors wide on our way into the Longhorn Saloon. I strode to the bar with Whiny shuffling behind me. The floor contained several well-worn tables and chairs supporting a cross-section of barroom miscreants. Two sad poker games silently kept participants leery of each other while one man sat alone at another table, sleeping with his face in a puddle of beer. Two cowhands snickered as a tipsy shop clerk shared what sounded like an off-color joke. All of the saloon customers looked like they needed a bath more than we did. The bar itself was built of rough pine—not ornate, but certainly utilitarian. A few cowboys tightened up, allowing us enough room to step in and give our drink order. I placed my right boot on the rail and smiled at the gap-toothed buffalo in the vest behind the bar. "Two milks," I said. Then I wondered, "Why the heck did I do that. I really could use a beer."

All eyes in the room turned toward us like we had scales and a rattle.

Following a short hesitation, the bartender turned, reached up into the cupboard and pulled down a pitcher of milk. "I keep this here just in case one of you types comes in."

"You types?" Whiny questioned.

He poured two glasses of the white liquid and slid them in front of us. I tossed a quarter in front of him.

"Do I gotta really drink this stuff?" Whiny asked me.

"You know, I don't understand it either. We've always ordered milk. Who does that? This is a saloon."

I lifted the glass to my lips and then my expression turned inside out as I spat the foul-tasting clotted gunk on the floor. "What in the...?"

"We don't get many milk drinkers in here," the bartender said with a wicked smile. "That pitcher has been sitting up in the cupboard for quite some time."

I put both hands on my guns and stepped back.

"Hold on Bucko," Whiny said. "Let's just order somethin' else."

I relaxed. "Okay, I'll have a…"

"We'll have two sarsaparillas," the old man said.

"What? I want a beer!"

"Now, Buck. We never drink—remember? If a child walks in here, we wouldn't want him to see us sipping strong intoxicants."

"If a child walks into this saloon, he needs his butt whipped. I want a beer!"

"Don't say 'butt'!"

The bartender placed two sarsaparillas in front of us and then leaned forward. "You two boys are kinda odd," he said. "I shoulda known when I saw your white hat and somewhat flamboyant attire."

"What?" I sputtered.

"If y'all are gonna continue to make a fuss, you might just wanta strut outta here and go down the street about a block to the Shorthorn Saloon. It might just be more appropriate to your tastes."

What felt like a grizzly bear's paw gripped my shoulder as a voice sounding like it came from the ocean's depths accompanied a hot, foul-smelling breath on the back of my neck. "Time to leave, milk drinker!"

"Already?" I thought. "The obligatory saloon fight?"

I was confused. In my past, I would always walk into a saloon for an innocent drink of milk. And, every time, I'd end up in a fight. I shouldn't have been surprised that it seemed to be happening again; only this time, for some reason it just didn't make sense.

I spun around to face the ugly giant just in time to feel his grizzly bear knuckles against my human jaw. As I flew backward over the bar, I said, "Holy crap! That hurt!"

"Did you just say 'crap'?" Whiny asked, while breaking a chair over the goliath's head.

I knew I had been in many barroom brawls, but I didn't remember ever feeling pain from a punch. I leaped to the top of the bar and jumped onto the big man's back, while Whiny seemed to be hitting the bartender with a mop. My opponent spun in a circle and, once again, I flew backward—

this time onto the top of a table, which broke under me. I knew I had him right where I wanted him. Jumping to my feet, I stepped directly in front of him, leaned back, and threw a hard right fist into the left side of his chin. He didn't move. My right arm felt like it had compressed to at least a foot shorter than it was before the punch.

Bear man grabbed me with both claws and threw me out the swinging doors. As I remember it, and that memory is a little fuzzy, I believe I landed on the other side of the street. I propped myself up on an elbow just in time to see Whiny hit the dirt right next to me.

"Why that condinged flip dip fooforah!" Whiny sputtered. "If I was only twenty years younger, I'da taken that moose apart a piece at a time."

I looked at my sidekick and shook my head slowly; and it hurt.

The sheriff smirked down at us. "You guys really shouldn't have picked a fight with Blackie Sage. He's a hard hombre."

"Ya fink tho?" I stammered through my swollen lips.

A short time later I stood in front of a wall mirror, combing my hair in our hotel room. I was bathed, shaved and wearing a clean, pressed gray cavalry shirt, crisp white bandana and sharp black pants. My two-gun belt hung over the back of a chair.

"What the heck is that?" I sputtered, while looking at a dark, swollen lump on the side of my face.

"That, Bucko, is a bruise," said Whiny, who was sitting at a small table, also dressed in clean clothes that looked exactly like the dirty ones he had been wearing earlier.

"I've never had one of those!" I exclaimed.

"Yepper, dagnabit," the bearded savant added, as he shoved a glop of some kind of mush from a bowl into his mouth, dribbling a bit onto his beard. "I've also never seen you lose a saloon fight before."

"Yeah. What's with that?"

"Maybe you didn't have a good enough breakfast," he answered, holding up a spoonful of whatever it was he was gobbling.

"What the blazes are you talkin' about?"

"Wheat Bloopers," he said with a big grin. "They're shot from cannons and packed with explosive energy."

"You're an idiot!" I spat. "Now I'm gonna go find that Blackie bum and put him down like a dog!"

"I don't know, Buck. He's kinda big. You might lose again. Maybe if you had a bowl of Wheat Bloopers...."

"I certainly won't lose if I bring a fencepost with me and bonk him from behind!"

"Oh, no, no, no, no, no," my irritating sidekick said. "Buck West never fights dirty!"

"The Buck West who never lost a fight never fought dirty," I responded. "This Buck West is gonna come from behind and bonk Blackie Sage into dithering senility!"

"But what if a child sees...?"

"You, and that fictitious child, need to mind your own damn business!"

"Flabbering mule flutes! You said the D-word!"

"Effinay! Now, let's saddle up and kick some ass!"

I felt fresh, alive and ready to take down that black hat. At the time, I didn't know what he was guilty of, besides thumpin' my hide. But I was sure that he was a no-good, dirty malefactor of some kind.

I strapped on my two custom-made, pearl-handled six-guns, grabbed my white Stetson and started for the stairs with my slightly confused side-kick shuffling along behind me, while he sputtered, "What the flip-flap, falderal, dag-nugget whip whap?" and other such noises.

I spotted my new nemesis right as we stepped out into the street. The big, burly bastard was standing looking down at an elderly man who, obviously, had been thrown into a water-filled horse trough. Blackie almost lost the cigar stub sticking out of his twisted mouth as he stood laughing with his hands on his hips. To match his hat, he wore a black leather vest, black pants tucked into black boots and a single revolver in a black holster on his right hip.

Several quaint but cowardly townspeople gathered to witness the excitement.

The old man gasped as he struggled to remove himself from the trough. His wet gray hair hung down and stuck to his face while he spit mouths full of muddy water. A lovely but flustered, raven-haired, beautiful woman scurried to his side and tried to pull him out. She wore a flower-print, floor-length dress that looked like an opera-house drape with three layers, including frilled tassels. Her collar covered her neck completely and was surrounded by a thin gold chain that held an ivory-carved silhouette locket. Her hat was a flower and feather-covered monstrosity that tilted on top of her thick black hair, which framed a face so bewitching it caused me to stand stone still and gawk.

"This is your last warning, Pop!" Blackie spat. "You'll either sell us your property and get out of town, or I'll bury you there! And then you'll never know what happens to your precious little daughter!"

"Yes!" I thought. "Blackie *is* a criminal! And this is where the hero steps in to save the day!"

"You animal!" the young lady exclaimed while kneeling next to her wet father. "You'll pay for this!" Blackie reached down and slapped her ornate chapeau off of her head and into the trough.

I stepped forward with both guns drawn. My legs were set wide and my eyes fixed on Sage. "You had enough fun, pig?"

Blackie spun to face me with his right hand set for a quick draw.

"Go ahead; reach for it," I suggested.

"So, it's the milk drinker. It looks to me like you didn't learn your lesson very well. Why don't you put down those guns and face me man to man?"

"Probably not a good idea," Whiny counseled, as several townspeople shook their heads in agreement.

"Oh, I learned my lesson. And, although it was a tad painful, I thank you. I don't plan on making that mistake again."

"You're yeller, ya dirty yeller, white-hat rat!"

"Maybe. Let's see how long *your* yeller stripe runs?" I smiled. "A big, dumb piece of crap like you never seems to be the brains behind land-grabs. You just do the dirty work. Who's your boss?"

Whiny leaned close to my ear and whispered, "There are two little girls in front of the barber shop. And you said 'crap' again." Several of the assembled locals gasped and covered their children's ears.

"I'm not answering any of your questions, funny boy," Sage stated. "And since I haven't reached for my guns, you won't shoot me."

"What makes you think I won't enable a little sunshine to warm your intestines, weasel butt?" Another gasp came from the crowd, as Whiny practically bit my ear when he whispered, "Don't say 'butt'!"

I held my left six-gun aimed at Sage's villainous head while I lowered my right revolver to point at his crotch. The blackguard's eyes bugged out and his jaw dropped. Our witnesses gasped again.

"Oh, you can't do that!" Whiny whined. "What's the matter with you, Buck? You've never shot anyone without them drawin' first."

"Hey!" I looked at my sidekick with a disapproving expression. "Go sit down!"

The assembled townspeople all had expressions on their faces that mirrored Sage's. Most of them were men in cowpuncher togs and women wearing long, heavy dresses with homemade bustles. A couple of men looked to either be bankers, attorneys or pickpockets while one guy's eyeshade gave away his occupation as an accountant. Some children had climbed up on their fathers' shoulders to get a better view of the excitement.

There was a hushed rumble of voices, which filtered into an unintelligible mumble. Oddly, I could hear other strange sounds coming from some place in the area. I heard a clatter, clicking and whirring that I just couldn't seem to place.

In complete contrast to the bug-eyed expressions of the townspeople, a middle-aged man wearing jodhpurs, eastern riding boots and a newsboy cap stood on the boardwalk frowning in my direction. I wondered if he was Sage's boss.

"It seems you don't want to answer any questions," I said to the sneering bad guy. "So, I guess it's my turn to say, last chance."

I counted to five, re-aimed my right pistol and fired. Sage's knee exploded, blasting bone, blood and flesh into dirt. He screamed and tumbled onto his face. Someone in our audience yelled, "What the...?" Whiny looked at me like I had just pulled down my pants and taken a dump in front of the town's church choir.

"What?" I asked him, while kicking Blackie's pistol out of his reach.

Sage groaned while Whiny helped the pretty lady pull the old man out of the trough.

"A bit excessive, don't you think?" the wet old man said to me.

"Hey," I answered a bit defensively. "I've been in Corriganville for almost an hour. I need to find out who gives this asshole his orders."

Whiny started to say something, but I gave him a "Don't you dare" look and he closed his mouth.

"I'm Pop Chaste," the old timer said. "And this is my daughter, Angelina."

The pretty girl stepped over Sage's twisted, bloody leg and took my hand. "Thank you very much for helping us."

"You're extremely welcome darlin'. But I'm not done with this rattlesnake. He's gonna tell me who's behind his attempt to take your land, and why."

"The why is easy," Pop said, while trying to straighten his wet suit. "I had spent years searchin' the foothills of my property for gold."

"Didja find gold?" a suddenly enthusiastic Whiny asked.

"Better," Pop answered. "I found a large natural spring that only runs along the surface of my land for about a hundred feet before dropping back into an underground river. Around here, that spring water is worth more than gold."

"No gold, huh?" Whiny leaned back against a hitching post.

"Then we only need to find out who is giving Blackie his nefarious orders," I said, turning back to the whimpering black-clad buffoon in the street. "Okay, Sage. Talk! Who's your boss?"

With mud streaked on his tear-stained face, Blackie looked up at me. "And if I don't tell you, you'll take out my other knee?"

"Oh, no," I said, while aiming both of my six-guns at his crotch.

"Flint Hart!" he hollered quickly.

"Why, Flint's a friend of mine," Pop said. "He's the town's only attorney."

"Surprise, surprise," Whiny said. "A crooked attorney. Who would have thought that could happen?"

I returned my guns to their holsters and turned to face the advancing sheriff. "You heard?"

"I did."

"Then take him away," I said. "We'll bring that crooked attorney in momentarily."

The big lawman and two volunteers struggled to carry the wounded villain toward the sheriff's office. "Someone get the doc to come over to the jail," the man with the star said.

"You know," Whiny offered. "Attorneys belong to the second oldest profession."

"And how do you know that?" Angelina asked.

"I read it in the good book," he answered, with a professorial smirk on his face. "It states categorically the very first time a man got a big-mouthed lawyer to fight his battles."

"I don't remember reading that part," Pop said.

"Surely you recall the story about Samson using the jawbone of an ass to smite his enemies."

The sound of a shot came from down the street near the sheriff's office. The lawman had fallen to the ground with his right hand on his left shoulder. An armed, black-hatted, mustached man wearing a gray suit stood on the boards in front of the law office across the street and fired another shot. This one caused Blackie to stop moaning, forever.

I jumped to my feet and drew my gun. With one shot, the crooked attorney bounced backward, his gun flying in the other direction. The sheriff ran to where Flint Hart was curled up on his side. "Good shootin', Buck."

"My pardner always just shoots the guns out of their hands," smiling Whiny proclaimed.

"Well, this time he got the gun out of the attorney's hand by shooting him through the wrist," the sheriff chuckled.

Whiny gave me a dirty look.

"Hey. I slipped. Nobody's perfect."

Angelina ran up and hugged me. "You're not going to leave, are you?"

"Naw," I answered, while pulling her closer to me. "I can stick around as long as you'd like."

"No you can't," Whiny said. "We gotta go."

"Don't listen to him," I told the beautiful young lady. "I'm yours."

And I lifted her slightly to press our lips together. For the first time, a tingling sensation coursed through my body. It was wonderful. I reached down with my hand and gripped Angelina Chaste by her left butt cheek.

Something made a slamming sound behind me. I turned to see the man with the newsboy cap and jodhpurs running toward me.

"That's it!" he yelled. "Cut!"

Then everything faded to black.

I must have been unconscious for some time. I don't even remember having dreamed. When I came to, I was facing the swinging saloon doors from the inside with my back to the bar. I saw a pair of boots walk up, pause and then the doors were pushed wide—exposing a very dusty Whiny. I smiled.

Then another dusty man entered and stood next to him. He was wearing my guns, gray cavalry shirt, dirty white bandana and large white Stetson. Only he was taller and better looking than me. The two of them walked to the bar and placed their right boot toes on the brass rail.

I didn't quite understand what was happening until I turned to face the bar—and the mirror behind it. My reflection showed that I had a gray streak in my hair, a pencil-thin black mustache on my upper lip and I was wearing a gambler's jacket, vest and black hat. My jaw dropped as I heard the big man place his order. "Two glasses of milk, please."

Editor's Note: When an author receives an unsolicited email asking for an interview, she can never know what to expect. How one may be portrayed, and what types of questions will be asked are two common concerns. Joni graciously agreed. An award-winning author, Joni has decades of experience in journalism, and is also one of the few female aircraft pilots of today. Welcome Joni M. Fisher!

ADVENTURES: It's more than a formality when I say it's our pleasure to have this interview with you. Thank you so much for your time.

In reading about you at your website (JoniMFisher.com), it looks like we may be from the same generation, or close. However, as a male, I could not have any idea what a girl in grade school, let's say, 30 or 40 years ago was going through. You mention that you had your sights set on going to college, but your guidance counselor had other ideas. Thankfully, you were a strong and determined girl at a young age. Where did you get your strength and courage, and did the idea ever cross your mind to give in, fall in line, and just do what's expected of you?

JF: Perhaps my strength and courage come from simple stubbornness. Generally, I followed the rules and behaved well as a child, except when confronted by something I found stupid. For example, in fourth grade, my friends and I led a week-long protest against a school policy. The policy dictated that girls had to wear dresses or skirts to school. I had no problem with that, but in the winter in Wisconsin, we had to wear pants to keep from freezing. At school, we were required to climb out of our pants and put them in our lockers, which meant we were sometimes late for class and always the last ones in the class after outside recess.

For a week, all the fourth-grade girls banded together to wear pants, no skirts or dresses. We knew our parents would be called and we'd be reprimanded, but we continued until the teacher met with the parents and changed the policy. Girls throughout grade school and middle school congratulated us and celebrated our win.

Rebellion can be a good thing under the right circumstances.

ADVENTURES: I'm not an impatient person by nature, but many times when it comes to culture, change seems to come about so slowly. What seems objectively good for everyone involved hits road blocks and gets dragged out it seems for decades. In what ways can you say culture has changed for the better for women?

JF: World culture has always valued men more than women. In the past decades, more women have entered careers as doctors, pilots, soldiers, lawyers, mechanics, law enforcement, and other male-dominated fields. Women hold seats in Congress and in the Supreme Court which means great progress.

While women have achieved a foothold of equality in some areas, they have lost ground in others. The recent trend toward allowing male-born transgenders to compete in women's sports is destroying women's sports. Notice how no born-female transgenders are demanding to compete in men's sports? Lately, even the words 'woman' and 'mother' are being neutered and erased by extremists. I laugh at those who demand the use of 'birthing-person' instead of mother. To date, no men have given birth, so what's the problem with acknowledging a mother as a woman?

And when it comes to crime, notice the use of passive verbs. A woman has been raped, not a man raped her. By using passive verbs, the male doesn't appear responsible or even present in committing the crime. We have a long way to go to achieve anything close to equality.

In my novels, I feature strong heroines whose lives are upended by a crime. The story details what the women do about the crime and none of them give up or wait around for a knight in shining armor to rescue them. We need more powerful women role models for the next generation.

ADVENTURES: Of course I have a dozen questions I could ask, but I'd like to let you have the floor. Before we close, is there anything you'd like to say? You may wish to address young people today, especially young women who may be wondering what road they should take.

JF: When I speak at colleges and writer's groups, I meet many young people trying to find their calling, their mission in life. I recommend a book called What Color Is Your Parachute? This book explores areas of skills and interests in broad categories and asks hundreds of questions that provoke deep thought. If you know you like working with people more than with things or ideas, then that's a start. By hashing through likes and dislikes, skills and abilities, you get to know who you are and who you want to become. The rest is finding a career or vocation that makes you happiest because, in the end, you want to look back at your life without regret.

Michael Jordan didn't become a great basketball player to get rich. He played because he loved everything about it from practice drills to competition. Because he loved what he did, he became great at it and the money followed.

Mother Theresa handled millions of dollars during her life in India and she did not seek fame. She used the money she got to care for the poor. She became famous and used her fame to reach wealthier donors to give more money to the poor. Her life of service made her happy.

Seeking fame or wealth is a life of frustration. There will never be enough to fill a void in the soul. Discover a life of joy. Fame and wealth might follow, but if it doesn't, it is still a life of joy.

Be sure to visit JoniMFisher.com for more.

Escape to your imagination with reading.
For our growing list of books, visit us at: OffBeatReads.com and be sure to subscribe so you never miss a release.
offbeat Reads
Always adventure in a book.

INTRODUCTION

WHEN WE THINK of vampires we think of Dracula, specifically the story by Bram Stoker from 1897. There are many areas of interest as well as questions regarding the original Stoker work. Scholars seem to mostly agree on where Stoker got his ideas for Dracula, though there is still debate. Did he take ideas from the very real Vlad the Impaler, from the 1400s? (The son of Voivode Vlad II; also known as Vlad Dracul and Vlad the Dragon, of Wallachia.) Stoker likely gathered inspiration from European folktales as well, and Jules Verne even wrote The Castle of the Carpathians—first published in 1892—approximately *five years before* Dracula released. Bits from this story could very well have entered Stoker's mind. Endless information exists, but we may never know all that formed the foundation for Stoker's blood-sucker.

However, in 1819, decades before Dracula and decades before Stoker was born in 1847, The Vampyre was published.

In the summer of 1816, freakish weather brought much rain and cooler temperatures (known as The year Without a Summer) to Europe. Sheltering inside a mansion, The Villa Diodati in Switzerland, the handsome Lord Byron and his physician Polidori were visited by three who dared the elements. The guests were Percy Bysshe Shelley, Mary Shelley (name Mary Wollstonecraft Godwin at the time) and Claire Clairmont.

Surely the monotony of circumstances got the best of them. Their confinement induced them to read from an anthology of German horror stories called Fantasmagoriana. Then came an idea: they would have a contest—most frightening story wins. Lord Byron, both Shelleys and Polidori took part. From this contest came Mary Shelley's Frankenstein, and the story Lord Byron concocted was the fodder for Polidori's The Vampyre.

The British, *The New Monthly Magazine*, published The Vampyre, at first attributing it to Lord Byron. In a letter to the editor, Polidori stated:

"...though the groundwork is certainly Lord Byron's, its development is mine".

Finally, though the coroner said Polidori died of natural causes (at age 25) in 1821, there is strong belief that the weight of gambling debts and depression caused Polidori to end his own life by ingesting an acid.

What follows is the original introduction by the author himself and, The Vampyre.

INTRODUCTION

BY THE AUTHOR
JOHN WILLIAM POLIDORI

THE SUPERSTITION UPON which this tale is founded is very general in the East. Among the Arabians it appears to be common: it did not, however, extend itself to the Greeks until after the establishment of Christianity; and it has only assumed its present form since the division of the Latin and Greek churches; at which time, the idea becoming prevalent, that a Latin body could not corrupt if buried in their territory, it gradually increased, and formed the subject of many wonderful stories, still extant, of the dead rising from their graves, and feeding upon the blood of the young and beautiful. In the West it spread, with some slight variation, all over Hungary, Poland, Austria, and Lorraine, where the belief existed, that vampyres nightly imbibed a certain portion of the blood of their victims, who became emaciated, lost their strength, and speedily died of consumptions; whilst these human blood-suckers fattened—and their veins became distended to such a state of repletion, as to cause the blood to flow from all the passages of their bodies, and even from the very pores of their skins.

In the London Journal, of March, 1732, is a curious, and, of course, credible account of a particular case of vampyrism, which is stated to have occurred at Madreyga, in Hungary. It appears, that upon an examination of the commander-in-chief and magistrates of the place, they positively and unanimously affirmed, that, about five years before, a certain Heyduke, named Arnold Paul, had been heard to say, that, at Cassovia, on the frontiers of the Turkish Servia, he had been tormented by a vampyre, but had found a way to rid himself of the evil, by eating some of the earth out of the vampyre's grave, and rubbing himself with his blood. This precaution, however, did not prevent him from becoming a vampyre[1] himself; for, about twenty or thirty days after his death and burial, many persons complained of having been tormented by him, and a deposition was made, that four persons had been deprived of life by his attacks. To prevent further mischief, the inhabitants having consulted their Hadagni,[2] took up the body, and found it (as is supposed to be usual in cases of vampyrism) fresh, and entirely free from corruption, and emitting at the mouth, nose, and ears, pure and florid blood. Proof having been thus obtained, they resorted to the accustomed remedy. A stake was driven entirely through the heart and body of Arnold Paul, at which he is reported to have cried out as dreadfully as if he had been alive. This done, they cut off his head, burned his body, and threw the ashes into his grave. The same measures were adopted with the corses of those persons who had previously died from vampyrism, lest they should, in their turn, become agents upon others who survived them.

This monstrous rodomontade is here related, because it seems better adapted to illustrate the subject of the present observations than any other instance which could be adduced. In many parts of Greece it is considered as a sort of punishment after death, for some heinous crime committed whilst in existence, that the deceased is not only doomed to vampyrise, but compelled to confine his infernal visitations solely to those beings he loved most while upon earth—those to whom he was bound by ties of kindred and affection.—A supposition alluded to in the "Giaour."

> *But first on earth, as Vampyre sent,*
> *Thy corse shall from its tomb be rent;*
> *Then ghastly haunt the native place,*
> *And suck the blood of all thy race;*
> *There from thy daughter, sister, wife,*
> *At midnight drain the stream of life;*
> *Yet loathe the banquet which perforce*
> *Must feed thy livid living corse,*
> *Thy victims, ere they yet expire,*
> *Shall know the demon for their sire;*
> *As cursing thee, thou cursing them,*
> *Thy flowers are withered on the stem.*

---

1. The universal belief is, that a person sucked by a vampyre becomes a vampyre himself, and sucks in his turn.
2. Chief bailiff.

But one that for thy crime must fall,
The youngest, best beloved of all,
Shall bless thee with a father's name—
That word shall wrap thy heart in flame!
Yet thou must end thy task and mark
Her cheek's last tinge—her eye's last spark,
And the last glassy glance must view
Which freezes o'er its lifeless blue;
Then with unhallowed hand shall tear
The tresses of her yellow hair,
Of which, in life a lock when shorn
Affection's fondest pledge was worn—
But now is borne away by thee
Memorial of thine agony!
Yet with thine own best blood shall drip;
Thy gnashing tooth, and haggard lip;
Then stalking to thy sullen grave,
Go—and with Gouls and Afrits rave,
Till these in horror shrink away
From spectre more accursed than they.

Mr. Southey has also introduced in his wild but beautiful poem of "Thalaba," the vampyre corse of the Arabian maid Oneiza, who is represented as having returned from the grave for the purpose of tormenting him she best loved whilst in existence. But this cannot be supposed to have resulted from the sinfulness of her life, she being pourtrayed throughout the whole of the tale as a complete type of purity and innocence. The veracious Tournefort gives a long account in his travels of several astonishing cases of vampyrism, to which he pretends to have been an eyewitness; and Calmet, in his great work upon this subject, besides a variety of anecdotes, and traditionary narratives illustrative of its effects, has put forth some learned dissertations, tending to prove it to be a classical, as well as barbarian error.

Many curious and interesting notices on this singularly horrible superstition might be added; though the present may suffice for the limits of a note, necessarily devoted to explanation, and which may now be concluded by merely remarking, that though the term Vampyre is the one in most general acceptation, there are several others synonymous with it, made use of in various parts of the world: as Vroucolocha, Vardoulacha, Goul, Broucoloka, &c.

THE VAMPYRE

JOHN WILLIAM POLIDORI

IT HAPPENED THAT in the midst of the dissipations attendant upon a London winter, there appeared at the various parties of the leaders of the ton a nobleman, more remarkable for his singularities, than his rank. He gazed upon the mirth around him, as if he could not participate therein. Apparently, the light laughter of the fair only attracted his attention, that he might by a look quell it, and throw fear into those breasts where thoughtlessness reigned. Those who felt this sensation of awe, could not explain whence it arose: some attributed it to the dead grey eye, which, fixing upon the object's face, did not seem to penetrate, and at one glance to pierce through to the inward workings of the heart; but fell upon the cheek with a leaden ray that weighed upon the skin it could not pass. His peculiarities caused him to be invited to every house; all wished to see him, and those who had been accustomed to violent excitement, and now felt the weight of ennui, were pleased at having something in their presence capable of engaging their attention. In spite of the deadly hue of his face, which never gained a warmer tint, either from the blush of modesty, or from the strong emotion of passion, though its form and outline were beautiful, many of the female hunters after notoriety attempted to win his attentions, and gain, at least, some marks of what they might term affection: Lady Mercer, who had been the mockery of every monster shewn in drawing-rooms since her marriage, threw herself in his way, and did all but put on the dress of a mountebank, to attract his notice:—though in vain:—when she stood before him, though his eyes were apparently fixed upon her's, still it seemed as if they were unperceived;—even her unappalled impudence was baffled, and she left the field. But though the common adultress could not influence even the guidance of his eyes, it was not that the female sex was indifferent to him: yet such was the apparent caution with which he spoke to the virtuous wife and innocent daughter, that few knew he ever addressed himself to females. He had, however, the reputation of a winning tongue; and whether it was that it even overcame the dread of his singular character, or that they were moved by his apparent hatred of vice, he was as often among those females who form the boast of their sex from their domestic virtues, as among those who sully it by their vices.

About the same time, there came to London a young gentleman of the name of Aubrey: he was an orphan left with an only sister in the possession of great wealth, by parents who died while he was yet in childhood. Left also to himself by guardians, who thought it their duty merely to take care of his fortune, while they relinquished the more important charge of his mind to the care of mercenary subalterns, he cultivated more his imagination than his judgment. He had, hence, that high romantic feeling of honour and candour, which daily ruins so many milliners' apprentices. He believed all to sympathise with virtue, and thought that vice was thrown in by Providence merely for the picturesque effect of the scene, as we see in romances: he thought that the misery of a cottage merely consisted in the vesting of clothes, which were as warm, but which were better adapted to the painter's eye by their irregular folds and various coloured patches. He thought, in fine, that the dreams of poets were the realities of life. He was handsome, frank, and rich: for these reasons, upon his entering into the gay circles, many mothers surrounded him, striving which should describe with least truth their languishing or romping favourites: the daughters at the same time, by their brightening countenances when he approached, and by their sparkling eyes, when he opened his lips, soon led him into false notions of his talents and his merit. Attached as he was to the romance of his solitary hours, he was startled at finding, that, except in the tallow and wax candles that flickered, not from the presence of a ghost, but from want of snuffing, there was no foundation in real life for any of that congeries of pleasing pictures and descriptions contained in those volumes, from which he had formed his study. Finding, however, some compensation in his gratified vanity, he was about to relinquish his dreams, when the extraordinary being we have above described, crossed him in his career.

He watched him; and the very impossibility of forming an idea of the character of a man entirely absorbed in himself, who gave few other signs of his observation of external objects, than the tacit assent to their existence, implied by the avoidance of their contact: allowing his imagination to picture every thing that flattered its propensity to extravagant ideas, he soon formed this object into the hero of a romance, and determined to observe the offspring of his fancy, rather than the person before him. He became acquainted with him, paid him attentions, and so far advanced upon his notice, that his presence was always recognised. He gradually learnt that Lord Ruthven's affairs were embarrassed, and soon found, from the notes of preparation in —— Street, that he was about to travel. Desirous of gaining some information respecting this singular character, who, till now, had only whetted his curiosity, he hinted to his guardians, that it was time for him to perform the tour, which for many generations has been thought necessary to enable the young to take some rapid steps in the career of vice towards putting themselves upon an equality with the aged, and not allowing them to appear as if fallen from the skies, whenever scandalous intrigues are mentioned as the subjects of pleasantry or of praise, according to the degree of skill shewn in carrying them on. They consented: and Aubrey immediately mentioning his intentions to Lord Ruthven, was surprised to receive from him a proposal to join him. Flattered by such a mark of esteem from him, who, apparently, had nothing in common with other men, he gladly accepted it, and in a few days they had passed the circling waters.

Hitherto, Aubrey had had no opportunity of studying Lord Ruthven's character, and now he found, that, though many more of his actions were exposed to his view, the results offered different conclusions from the apparent motives to his conduct. His companion was profuse in his liberality;—the idle, the vagabond, and the beggar, received from his hand more than enough to relieve their immediate wants. But Aubrey could not avoid remarking, that it was not upon the virtuous, reduced to indigence by the misfortunes attendant even upon virtue, that he bestowed his alms;—these were sent from the door with hardly suppressed sneers; but when the profligate came to ask something, not to relieve his wants, but to allow him to wallow in his lust, or to sink him still deeper in his iniquity, he was sent away with rich charity. This was, however, attributed by him to the greater importunity of the vicious, which generally prevails over the retiring bashfulness of the virtuous indigent. There was one circumstance about the charity of his Lordship, which was still more impressed upon his mind: all those upon whom it was bestowed, inevitably found that there was a curse upon it, for they were all either led to the scaffold, or sunk to the lowest and the most abject misery. At Brussels and other towns through which they passed, Aubrey was surprized at the apparent eagerness with which his companion sought for the centres of all fashionable vice; there he entered into all the spirit of the faro table: he betted, and always gambled with success, except where the known sharper was his antagonist, and then he lost even more than he gained; but it was always with the same unchanging face, with which he generally watched the society around: it was not, however, so when he encountered the rash youthful novice, or the luckless father of a numerous family; then his very wish seemed fortune's law—this apparent abstractedness of mind was laid aside, and his eyes sparkled with more fire than that of the cat whilst dallying with the half-dead mouse. In every town, he left the formerly affluent youth, torn from the circle he adorned, cursing, in the solitude of a dungeon, the fate that had drawn him within the reach of this fiend; whilst many a father sat frantic, amidst the speaking looks of mute hungry children, without a single farthing of his late immense wealth, wherewith to buy even sufficient to satisfy their present craving. Yet he took no money from the gambling table; but immediately lost, to the ruiner of many, the last gilder he had just snatched from the convulsive grasp of the innocent: this might but be the result of a certain degree of knowledge, which was not, however, capable of combating the cunning of the more experienced. Aubrey often wished to represent this to his friend, and beg him to resign that charity and pleasure which proved the ruin of all, and did not tend to his own profit;—but he delayed it—for each day he hoped his friend would give him some opportunity of speaking frankly and openly to him; however, this never occurred. Lord Ruthven in his carriage, and amidst the various wild and rich scenes of nature, was always the same: his eye spoke less than his lip; and though Aubrey was near the object of his curiosity, he obtained no greater gratification from it than the constant excitement of vainly wishing to break that mystery, which to his exalted imagination began to assume the appearance of something supernatural.

They soon arrived at Rome, and Aubrey for a time lost sight of his companion; he left him in daily attendance upon the morning circle of an Italian countess, whilst he went in search of the memorials of another almost deserted city. Whilst he was thus engaged, letters arrived from

England, which he opened with eager impatience; the first was from his sister, breathing nothing but affection; the others were from his guardians, the latter astonished him; if it had before entered into his imagination that there was an evil power resident in his companion, these seemed to give him sufficient reason for the belief. His guardians insisted upon his immediately leaving his friend, and urged, that his character was dreadfully vicious, for that the possession of irresistible powers of seduction, rendered his licentious habits more dangerous to society. It had been discovered, that his contempt for the adultress had not originated in hatred of her character; but that he had required, to enhance his gratification, that his victim, the partner of his guilt, should be hurled from the pinnacle of unsullied virtue, down to the lowest abyss of infamy and degradation: in fine, that all those females whom he had sought, apparently on account of their virtue, had, since his departure, thrown even the mask aside, and had not scrupled to expose the whole deformity of their vices to the public gaze.

Aubrey determined upon leaving one, whose character had not yet shown a single bright point on which to rest the eye. He resolved to invent some plausible pretext for abandoning him altogether, purposing, in the mean while, to watch him more closely, and to let no slight circumstances pass by unnoticed. He entered into the same circle, and soon perceived, that his Lordship was endeavouring to work upon the inexperience of the daughter of the lady whose house he chiefly frequented. In Italy, it is seldom that an unmarried female is met with in society; he was therefore obliged to carry on his plans in secret; but Aubrey's eye followed him in all his windings, and soon discovered that an assignation had been appointed, which would most likely end in the ruin of an innocent, though thoughtless girl. Losing no time, he entered the apartment of Lord Ruthven, and abruptly asked him his intentions with respect to the lady, informing him at the same time that he was aware of his being about to meet her that very night. Lord Ruthven answered, that his intentions were such as he supposed all would have upon such an occasion; and upon being pressed whether he intended to marry her, merely laughed. Aubrey retired; and, immediately writing a note, to say, that from that moment he must decline accompanying his Lordship in the remainder of their proposed tour, he ordered his servant to seek other apartments, and calling upon the mother of the lady, informed her of all he knew, not only with regard to her daughter, but also concerning the character of his Lordship. The assignation was prevented. Lord Ruthven next day merely sent his servant to notify his complete assent to a separation; but did not hint any suspicion of his plans having been foiled by Aubrey's interposition.

Having left Rome, Aubrey directed his steps towards Greece, and crossing the Peninsula, soon found himself at Athens. He then fixed his residence in the house of a Greek; and soon occupied himself in tracing the faded records of ancient glory upon monuments that apparently, ashamed of chronicling the deeds of freemen only before slaves, had hidden themselves beneath the sheltering soil or many coloured lichen. Under the same roof as himself, existed a being, so beautiful and delicate, that she might have formed the model for a painter wishing to pourtray on canvass the promised hope of the faithful in Mahomet's paradise, save that her eyes spoke too much mind for any one to think she could belong to those who had no souls. As she danced upon the plain, or tripped along the mountain's side, one would have thought the gazelle a poor type of her beauties; for who would have exchanged her eye, apparently the eye of animated nature, for that sleepy luxurious look of the animal suited but to the taste of an epicure. The light step of Ianthe often accompanied Aubrey in his search after antiquities, and often would the unconscious girl, engaged in the pursuit of a Kashmere butterfly, show the whole beauty of her form, floating as it were upon the wind, to the eager gaze of him, who forgot the letters he had just decyphered upon an almost effaced tablet, in the contemplation of her sylph-like figure. Often would her tresses falling, as she flitted around, exhibit in the sun's ray such delicately brilliant and swiftly fading hues, it might well excuse the forgetfulness of the antiquary, who let escape from his mind the very object he had before thought of vital importance to the proper interpretation of a passage in Pausanias. But why attempt to describe charms which all feel, but none can appreciate?—It was innocence, youth, and beauty, unaffected by crowded drawing-rooms and stifling balls. Whilst he drew those remains of which he wished to preserve a memorial for his future hours, she would stand by, and watch the magic effects of his pencil, in tracing the scenes of her native place; she would then describe to him the circling dance upon the open plain, would paint, to him in all the glowing colours of youthful memory, the marriage pomp she remembered viewing in her infancy; and then, turning to subjects that had evidently made a greater impression upon her mind, would tell him all the supernatural tales of her nurse. Her earnestness and apparent belief of what she narrated, excited the interest even of Aubrey; and often as she told him the tale of the living vampyre, who had passed years amidst his friends, and dearest ties, forced every year, by feeding upon the life of a lovely female to prolong his existence for the ensuing months, his blood would run cold, whilst he attempted to laugh her out of such idle and horrible fantasies; but Ianthe cited to him the names of old men, who had at last detected one living among themselves, after several of their near relatives and children had been found marked with the stamp of the fiend's appetite; and when she found him so incredulous, she begged of him to believe her, for it had been, remarked, that those who had dared to question their existence, always had some proof given, which obliged them, with grief and heartbreaking, to confess it was true. She detailed to him the traditional appearance of these monsters, and his horror was increased, by hearing a pretty accurate description of Lord Ruthven; he, however, still persisted in persuading her, that there could be no truth in her fears, though at the same time he wondered at the many coincidences which had all tended to excite a belief in the supernatural power of Lord Ruthven.

Aubrey began to attach himself more and more to Ianthe; her innocence, so contrasted with all the affected virtues of the women among whom he had sought for his vision of romance, won his heart; and while he ridiculed the idea of a young man of English habits, marrying an uneducated Greek girl, still he found himself more and more attached to the almost fairy form before him. He would tear himself at times from her, and, forming a plan for some antiquarian research, he would depart, determined not to return until his object was attained; but he always found it impossible to fix his attention upon the ruins around him, whilst in his mind he retained an image that seemed alone the rightful possessor of his thoughts. Ianthe was unconscious of his love, and was ever the same frank infantile being he had first known. She always seemed to part from him with reluctance; but it was because she had no longer any one with whom she could visit her favourite haunts, whilst her guardian was occupied in sketching or uncovering some fragment which had yet escaped the destructive hand of time. She had appealed to her parents on the subject of Vampyres, and they both, with several present, affirmed their existence, pale with horror at the very name. Soon after, Aubrey determined to proceed upon one of his excursions, which was to detain him for a few hours; when they heard the name of the place, they all at once begged of him not to return at night, as he must necessarily pass through a wood, where no Greek would ever remain, after the day had closed, upon any consideration. They described it as the resort of the vampyres in their nocturnal orgies, and denounced the most heavy evils as impending upon him who dared to cross their path. Aubrey made light of their representations, and tried to laugh them out of the idea; but when he saw them shudder at his daring thus to mock a superior, infernal power, the very name of which apparently made their blood freeze, he was silent.

Next morning Aubrey set off upon his excursion unattended; he was surprised to observe the melancholy face of his host, and was concerned to find that his words, mocking the belief of those horrible fiends, had inspired them with such terror. When he was about to depart, Ianthe came to the side of his horse, and earnestly begged of him to return, ere night allowed the power of these beings to be put in action;—he promised. He was, however, so occupied in his research, that he did not perceive that day-light would soon end, and that in the horizon there was one of those specks which, in the warmer climates, so rapidly gather into a tremendous mass, and pour all their rage upon the devoted country.— He at last, however, mounted his horse, determined to make up by speed for his delay: but it was too late. Twilight, in these southern climates, is almost unknown; immediately the sun sets, night begins: and ere he had advanced far, the power of the storm was above—its echoing thunders had scarcely an interval of rest—its thick heavy rain forced its way through the canopying foliage, whilst the blue forked lightning seemed to fall and radiate at his very feet. Suddenly his horse took fright, and he was carried with dreadful rapidity through the entangled forest. The animal at last, through fatigue, stopped, and he found, by the glare of lightning, that he was in the neighbourhood of a hovel that hardly lifted itself up from the masses of dead leaves and brushwood which surrounded it. Dismounting, he approached, hoping to find some one to guide him to the town, or at least trusting to obtain shelter from the pelting of the storm. As he approached, the thunders, for a moment silent, allowed him to hear the dreadful shrieks of a woman mingling with the stifled, exultant mockery of a laugh, continued in one almost unbroken sound;—he was startled: but, roused by the thunder which again rolled over his head, he, with a sudden effort, forced open the door of the hut. He found him-self in utter darkness: the sound, however, guided him. He was appar-ently unperceived; for, though he called, still the sounds continued, and no notice was taken of him. He found himself in contact with some one, whom he immediately seized; when a voice cried, "Again baffled!" to which a loud laugh succeeded; and he felt himself grappled by one whose strength seemed superhuman: determined to sell his life as dearly as he could, he struggled; but it was in vain: he was lifted from his feet and hurled with enormous force against the ground:—his enemy threw him-self upon him, and kneeling upon his breast, had placed his hands upon his throat—when the glare of many torches penetrating through the hole that gave light in the day, disturbed him;—he instantly rose, and, leav-ing his prey, rushed through the door, and in a moment the crashing of the branches, as he broke through the wood, was no longer heard. The storm was now still; and Aubrey, incapable of moving, was soon heard by those without. They entered; the light of their torches fell upon the mud walls, and the thatch loaded on every individual straw with heavy flakes of soot. At the desire of Aubrey they searched for her who had attracted him by her cries; he was again left in darkness; but what was his horror, when the light of the torches once more burst upon him, to perceive the airy form of his fair conductress brought in a lifeless corse. He shut his eyes, hoping that it was but a vision arising from his disturbed imagina-tion; but he again saw the same form, when he unclosed them, stretched by his side. There was no colour upon her cheek, not even upon her lip; yet there was a stillness about her face that seemed almost as attaching as the life that once dwelt there:—upon her neck and breast was blood, and upon her throat were the marks of teeth having opened the vein:—to this the men pointed, crying, simultaneously struck with horror, "A Vampyre! a Vampyre!" A litter was quickly formed, and Aubrey was laid by the side of her who had lately been to him the object of so many bright and fairy visions, now fallen with the flower of life that had died within her. He knew not what his thoughts were—his mind was benumbed and seemed to shun reflection, and take refuge in vacancy—he held almost uncon-sciously in his hand a naked dagger of a particular construction, which had been found in the hut. They were soon met by different parties who had been engaged in the search of her whom a mother had missed. Their lamentable cries, as they approached the city, forewarned the parents of some dreadful catastrophe. —To describe their grief would be impossible; but when they ascertained the cause of their child's death, they looked at Aubrey, and pointed to the corse. They were inconsolable; both died broken-hearted.

Aubrey being put to bed was seized with a most violent fever, and was often delirious; in these intervals he would call upon Lord Ruthven and upon Ianthe—by some unaccountable combination he seemed to beg of his former companion to spare the being he loved. At other times he would imprecate maledictions upon his head, and curse him as her destroyer. Lord Ruthven, chanced at this time to arrive at Athens, and, from whatever motive, upon hearing of the state of Aubrey, immediately placed himself in the same house, and became his constant attendant. When the latter recovered from his delirium, he was horrified and startled at the sight of him whose image he had now combined with that of a Vampyre; but Lord Ruthven, by his kind words, implying almost repentance for the fault that had caused their separation, and still more by the attention, anxiety, and care which he showed, soon reconciled him to his presence. His lordship seemed quite changed; he no longer appeared that apathetic being who had so astonished Aubrey; but as soon as his convalescence began to be rapid, he again gradually retired into the same state of mind, and Aubrey perceived no difference from the former man, except that at times he was surprised to meet his gaze fixed intently upon him, with a smile of malicious exultation playing upon his lips: he knew not why, but this smile haunted him. During the last stage of the invalid's recovery, Lord Ruthven was apparently engaged in watching the tideless waves raised by the cooling breeze, or in marking the progress of those orbs, circling, like our world, the moveless sun;—indeed, he appeared to wish to avoid the eyes of all.

Aubrey's mind, by this shock, was much weakened, and that elasticity of spirit which had once so distinguished him now seemed to have fled for ever. He was now as much a lover of solitude and silence as Lord Ruthven; but much as he wished for solitude, his mind could not find it in the neighbourhood of Athens; if he sought it amidst the ruins he had formerly frequented, Ianthe's form stood by his side—if he sought it in the woods, her light step would appear wandering amidst the underwood, in quest of the modest violet; then suddenly turning round, would show, to his wild imagination, her pale face and wounded throat, with a meek smile upon her lips. He determined to fly scenes, every feature of which created such bitter associations in his mind. He proposed to Lord Ruthven, to whom he held himself bound by the tender care he had taken of him during his illness, that they should visit those parts of Greece neither had yet seen. They travelled in every direction, and sought every spot to which a recollection could be attached: but though they thus hastened from place to place, yet they seemed not to heed what they gazed upon. They heard much of robbers, but they gradually began to slight these reports, which they imagined were only the invention of individuals, whose interest it was to excite the generosity of those whom they defended from pretended dangers. In consequence of thus neglecting the advice of the inhabitants, on one occasion they travelled with only a few guards, more to serve as guides than as a defence. Upon entering, however, a narrow defile, at the bottom of which was the bed of a torrent, with large masses of rock brought down from the neighbouring precipices, they had reason to repent their negligence; for scarcely were the whole of the party engaged in the narrow pass, when they were startled by the whistling of bullets close to their heads, and by the echoed report of several guns. In an instant their guards had left them, and, placing themselves behind rocks, had begun to fire in the direction whence the report came. Lord Ruthven and Aubrey, imitating their example, retired for a moment behind the sheltering turn of the defile: but ashamed of being thus detained by a foe, who with insulting shouts bade them advance, and being exposed to unresisting slaughter, if any of the robbers should climb above and take them in the rear, they determined at once to rush forward in search of the enemy. Hardly had they lost the shelter of the rock, when Lord Ruthven received a shot in the shoulder, which brought him to the ground. Aubrey hastened to his assistance; and, no longer heeding the contest or his own peril, was soon surprised by seeing the robbers' faces around him—his guards having, upon Lord Ruthven's being wounded, immediately thrown up their arms and surrendered.

By promises of great reward, Aubrey soon induced them to convey his wounded friend to a neighbouring cabin; and having agreed upon a ransom, he was no more disturbed by their presence—they being content merely to guard the entrance till their comrade should return with the promised sum, for which he had an order. Lord Ruthven's strength rapidly decreased; in two days mortification ensued, and death seemed advancing with hasty steps. His conduct and appearance had not changed; he seemed as unconscious of pain as he had been of the objects about him: but towards the close of the last evening, his mind became apparently uneasy, and his eye often fixed upon Aubrey, who was induced to offer his assistance with more than usual earnestness—"Assist me! you may save me—you may do more than that—I mean not my life, I heed the death of my existence as little as that of the passing day; but you may save my honour, your friend's honour."—"How? tell me how? I would do any thing," replied Aubrey.—"I need but little—my life ebbs apace—I cannot explain the whole—but if you would conceal all you know of me, my honour were free from stain in the world's mouth—and if my death were unknown for some time in England—I—I—but life."—"It shall not be known."—"Swear!" cried the dying man, raising himself with exultant violence, "Swear by all your soul reveres, by all your nature fears, swear that, for a year and a day you will not impart your knowledge of my crimes or death to any living being in any way, whatever may happen, or whatever you may see."—His eyes seemed bursting from their sockets: "I swear!" said Aubrey; he sunk laughing upon his pillow, and breathed no more.

Aubrey retired to rest, but did not sleep; the many circumstances attending his acquaintance with this man rose upon his mind, and he knew not why; when he remembered his oath a cold shivering came over him, as if from the presentiment of something horrible awaiting him. Rising early in the morning, he was about to enter the hovel in which he had left the corpse, when a robber met him, and informed him that it was no longer there, having been conveyed by himself and comrades, upon his retiring, to the pinnacle of a neighbouring mount, according to a promise they had given his lordship, that it should be exposed to the first cold ray of the moon that rose after his death. Aubrey astonished, and taking several of the men, determined to go and bury it upon the spot where it lay. But, when he had mounted to the summit he found no trace of either the corpse or the clothes, though the robbers swore they pointed out the identical rock on which they had laid the body. For a time his mind was bewildered in conjectures, but he at last returned, convinced that they had buried the corpse for the sake of the clothes.

Weary of a country in which he had met with such terrible misfortunes, and in which all apparently conspired to heighten that superstitious melancholy that had seized upon his mind, he resolved to leave it, and soon arrived at Smyrna. While waiting for a vessel to convey him to Otranto, or to Naples, he occupied himself in arranging those effects he had with him belonging to Lord Ruthven. Amongst other things there was a case containing several weapons of offence, more or less adapted to ensure the death of the victim. There were several daggers and ataghans. Whilst turning them over, and examining their curious forms, what was his surprise at finding a sheath apparently ornamented in the same style as the dagger discovered in the fatal hut—he shuddered—hastening to gain further proof, he found the weapon, and his horror may be imagined when he discovered that it fitted, though peculiarly shaped, the sheath he held in his hand. His eyes seemed to need no further certainty—they seemed gazing to be bound to the dagger; yet still he wished to disbelieve; but the particular form, the same varying tints upon the haft and sheath were alike in splendour on both, and left no room for doubt; there were also drops of blood on each.

He left Smyrna, and on his way home, at Rome, his first inquiries were concerning the lady he had attempted to snatch from Lord Ruthven's seductive arts. Her parents were in distress, their fortune ruined, and she had not been heard of since the departure of his lordship. Aubrey's mind became almost broken under so many repeated horrors; he was afraid that this lady had fallen a victim to the destroyer of Ianthe. He became morose and silent; and his only occupation consisted in urging the speed of the postilions, as if he were going to save the life of some one he held dear. He arrived at Calais; a breeze, which seemed obedient to his will, soon wafted him to the English shores; and he hastened to the mansion of his fathers, and there, for a moment, appeared to lose, in the embraces and caresses of his sister, all memory of the past. If she before, by her infantine caresses, had gained his affection, now that the woman began to appear, she was still more attaching as a companion.

Miss Aubrey had not that winning grace which gains the gaze and applause of the drawing-room assemblies. There was none of that light brilliancy which only exists in the heated atmosphere of a crowded apartment. Her blue eye was never lit up by the levity of the mind beneath. There was a melancholy charm about it which did not seem to arise from misfortune, but from some feeling within, that appeared to indicate a soul conscious of a brighter realm. Her step was not that light footing, which strays where'er a butterfly or a colour may attract—it was sedate and pensive. When alone, her face was never brightened by the smile of joy; but when her brother breathed to her his affection, and would in her presence forget those griefs she knew destroyed his rest, who would have exchanged her smile for that of the voluptuary? It seemed as if those eyes,—that face were then playing in the light of their own native sphere. She was yet only eighteen, and had not been presented to the world, it having been thought by her guardians more fit that her presentation should be delayed until her brother's return from the continent, when he might be her protector. It was now, therefore, resolved that the next drawing-room, which was fast approaching, should be the epoch of her entry into the "busy scene." Aubrey would rather have remained in the mansion of his fathers, and fed upon the melancholy which overpowered him. He could not feel interest about the frivolities of fashionable strangers, when his mind had been so torn by the events he had witnessed; but he determined to sacrifice his own comfort to the protection of his sister. They soon arrived in town, and prepared for the next day, which had been announced as a drawing-room.

The crowd was excessive—a drawing-room had not been held for a long time, and all who were anxious to bask in the smile of royalty, hastened thither. Aubrey was there with his sister. While he was standing in a corner by himself, heedless of all around him, engaged in the remembrance that the first time he had seen Lord Ruthven was in that very place—he felt himself suddenly seized by the arm, and a voice he recognized too well, sounded in his ear—"Remember your oath." He had hardly courage to turn, fearful of seeing a spectre that would blast him, when he perceived, at a little distance, the same figure which had attracted his notice on this spot upon his first entry into society. He gazed till his limbs almost refusing to bear their weight, he was obliged to take the arm of a friend, and forcing a passage through the crowd, he threw himself into his carriage, and was driven home. He paced the room with hurried steps, and fixed his hands upon his head, as if he were afraid his thoughts were bursting from his brain. Lord Ruthven again before him—circumstances started up in dreadful array—the dagger—his oath.—He roused himself, he could not believe it possible—the dead rise again!—He thought his imagination had conjured up the image his mind was resting upon. It was impossible that it could be real—he determined, therefore, to go again into society; for though he attempted to ask concerning

Lord Ruthven, the name hung upon his lips, and he could not succeed in gaining information. He went a few nights after with his sister to the assembly of a near relation. Leaving her under the protection of a matron, he retired into a recess, and there gave himself up to his own devouring thoughts. Perceiving, at last, that many were leaving, he roused himself, and entering another room, found his sister surrounded by several, apparently in earnest conversation; he attempted to pass and get near her, when one, whom he requested to move, turned round, and revealed to him those features he most abhorred. He sprang forward, seized his sister's arm, and, with hurried step, forced her towards the street: at the door he found himself impeded by the crowd of servants who were waiting for their lords; and while he was engaged in passing them, he again heard that voice whisper close to him—"Remember your oath!"—He did not dare to turn, but, hurrying his sister, soon reached home.

Aubrey became almost distracted. If before his mind had been absorbed by one subject, how much more completely was it engrossed, now that the certainty of the monster's living again pressed upon his thoughts. His sister's attentions were now unheeded, and it was in vain that she intreated him to explain to her what had caused his abrupt conduct. He only uttered a few words, and those terrified her. The more he thought, the more he was bewildered. His oath startled him;—was he then to allow this monster to roam, bearing ruin upon his breath, amidst all he held dear, and not avert its progress? His very sister might have been touched by him. But even if he were to break his oath, and disclose his suspicions, who would believe him? He thought of employing his own hand to free the world from such a wretch; but death, he remembered, had been already mocked. For days he remained in this state; shut up in his room, he saw no one, and ate only when his sister came, who, with eyes streaming with tears, besought him, for her sake, to support nature. At last, no longer capable of bearing stillness and solitude, he left his house, roamed from street to street, anxious to fly that image which haunted him. His dress became neglected, and he wandered, as often exposed to the noon-day sun as to the midnight damps. He was no longer to be recognized; at first he returned with the evening to the house; but at last he laid him down to rest wherever fatigue overtook him. His sister, anxious for his safety, employed people to follow him; but they were soon distanced by him who fled from a pursuer swifter than any—from thought.

His conduct, however, suddenly changed. Struck with the idea that he left by his absence the whole of his friends, with a fiend amongst them, of whose presence they were unconscious, he determined to enter again into society, and watch him closely, anxious to forewarn, in spite of his oath, all whom Lord Ruthven approached with intimacy. But when he entered into a room, his haggard and suspicious looks were so striking, his inward shudderings so visible, that his sister was at last obliged to beg of him to abstain from seeking, for her sake, a society which affected him so strongly. When, however, remonstrance proved unavailing, the guardians thought proper to interpose, and, fearing that his mind was becoming alienated, they thought it high time to resume again that trust which had been before imposed upon them by Aubrey's parents.

Desirous of saving him from the injuries and sufferings he had daily encountered in his wanderings, and of preventing him from exposing to the general eye those marks of what they considered folly, they engaged a physician to reside in the house, and take constant care of him. He hardly appeared to notice it, so completely was his mind absorbed by one terrible subject. His incoherence became at last so great, that he was confined to his chamber. There he would often lie for days, incapable of being roused. He had become emaciated, his eyes had attained a glassy lustre;— the only sign of affection and recollection remaining displayed itself upon the entry of his sister; then he would sometimes start, and, seizing her hands, with looks that severely afflicted her, he would desire her not to touch him. "Oh, do not touch him—if your love for me is aught, do not go near him!" When, however, she inquired to whom he referred, his only answer was, "True! true!" and again he sank into a state, whence not even she could rouse him. This lasted many months: gradually, however, as the year was passing, his incoherences became less frequent, and his mind threw off a portion of its gloom, whilst his guardians observed, that several times in the day he would count upon his fingers a definite number, and then smile.

The time had nearly elapsed, when, upon the last day of the year, one of his guardians entering his room, began to converse with his physician upon the melancholy circumstance of Aubrey's being in so awful a situation, when his sister was going next day to be married. Instantly Aubrey's attention was attracted; he asked anxiously to whom. Glad of this mark of returning intellect, of which they feared he had been deprived, they men-

tioned the name of the Earl of Marsden. Thinking this was a young Earl whom he had met with in society, Aubrey seemed pleased, and astonished them still more by his expressing his intention to be present at the nuptials, and desiring to see his sister. They answered not, but in a few minutes his sister was with him. He was apparently again capable of being affected by the influence of her lovely smile; for he pressed her to his breast, and kissed her cheek, wet with tears, flowing at the thought of her brother's being once more alive to the feelings of affection. He began to speak with all his wonted warmth, and to congratulate her upon her marriage with a person so distinguished for rank and every accomplishment; when he suddenly perceived a locket upon her breast; opening it, what was his surprise at beholding the features of the monster who had so long influenced his life. He seized the portrait in a paroxysm of rage, and trampled it under foot. Upon her asking him why he thus destroyed the resemblance of her future husband, he looked as if he did not understand her—then seizing her hands, and gazing on her with a frantic expression of countenance, he bade her swear that she would never wed this monster, for he—
— But he could not advance—it seemed as if that voice again bade him remember his oath—he turned suddenly round, thinking Lord Ruthven was near him but saw no one. In the meantime the guardians and physician, who had heard the whole, and thought this was but a return of his disorder, entered, and forcing him from Miss Aubrey, desired her to leave him. He fell upon his knees to them, he implored, he begged of them to delay but for one day. They, attributing this to the insanity they imagined had taken possession of his mind, endeavoured to pacify him, and retired.

Lord Ruthven had called the morning after the drawing-room, and had been refused with every one else. When he heard of Aubrey's ill health, he readily understood himself to be the cause of it; but when he learned that he was deemed insane, his exultation and pleasure could hardly be concealed from those among whom he had gained this information. He hastened to the house of his former companion, and, by constant attendance, and the pretence of great affection for the brother and interest in his fate, he gradually won the ear of Miss Aubrey. Who could resist his power? His tongue had dangers and toils to recount—could speak of himself as of an individual having no sympathy with any being on the crowded earth, save with her to whom he addressed himself;—could tell how, since he knew her, his existence, had begun to seem worthy of preservation, if it were merely that he might listen to her soothing accents;—in fine, he knew so well how to use the serpent's art, or such was the will of fate, that he gained her affections. The title of the elder branch falling at length to him, he obtained an important embassy, which served as an excuse for hastening the marriage, (in spite of her brother's deranged state,) which was to take place the very day before his departure for the continent.

Aubrey, when he was left by the physician and his guardians, attempted to bribe the servants, but in vain. He asked for pen and paper; it was given him; he wrote a letter to his sister, conjuring her, as she valued her own happiness, her own honour, and the honour of those now in the grave, who once held her in their arms as their hope and the hope of their house, to delay but for a few hours that marriage, on which he denounced the most heavy curses. The servants promised they would deliver it; but giving it to the physician, he thought it better not to harass any more the mind of Miss Aubrey by, what he considered, the ravings of a maniac. Night passed on without rest to the busy inmates of the house; and Aubrey heard, with a horror that may more easily be conceived than described, the notes of busy preparation. Morning came, and the sound of carriages broke upon his ear. Aubrey grew almost frantic. The curiosity of the servants at last overcame their vigilance, they gradually stole away, leaving him in the custody of an helpless old woman. He seized the opportunity, with one bound was out of the room, and in a moment found himself in the apartment where all were nearly assembled. Lord Ruthven was the first to perceive him: he immediately approached, and, taking his arm by force, hurried him from the room, speechless with rage. When on the staircase, Lord Ruthven whispered in his ear—"Remember your oath, and know, if not my bride to day, your sister is dishonoured. Women are frail!" So saying, he pushed him towards his attendants, who, roused by the old woman, had come in search of him. Aubrey could no longer support himself; his rage not finding vent, had broken a blood-vessel, and he was conveyed to bed. This was not mentioned to his sister, who was not present when he entered, as the physician was afraid of agitating her. The marriage was solemnized, and the bride and bridegroom left London.

Aubrey's weakness increased; the effusion of blood produced symptoms of the near approach of death. He desired his sister's guardians might be called, and when the midnight hour had struck, he related composedly what the reader has perused—he died immediately after.

The guardians hastened to protect Miss Aubrey; but when they arrived, it was too late. Lord Ruthven had disappeared, and Aubrey's sister had glutted the thirst of a VAMPYRE!

1942 in Nyssa, Oregon: on their weekly trip to town, a Japanese-American farm worker and child enjoy an ice cream soda.

DETECTIVE WOLFRAM
GETS A CASE

BY MICHAEL BRIAN

The bell tinkled as the door to Emery Marigold's bookshop opened. He looked up.

His jaw dropped so quickly he'd be chewing crooked for days. The dame standing in his doorway was so hot, she could melt a cheese sandwich from across the room. Her gams practically begged to be admired. But she had trouble written all over her face.

"Excuse me? Hello?"

"Huh?" Marigold looked up, embarrassed. He had been narrating again. Ever since reading his first novel by Raymond Chandler, it became a habit to narrate everyday moments in the tone of a gritty detective. He felt it gave these scenes more importance.

"I need help finding a book," the lady said.

"You've come to the right place, doll," he said, recovering quickly. His old wooden chair creaked as he stood up. "Can you provide any details about the book in question?"

As she talked, he scribbled down notes in a little red notepad he carried in his breast pocket. It was an unnecessary formality, as he knew what book was being described. Still, he liked to go through the process. He shut the notebook dramatically.

"I cracked the case!" he announced and directed her to a bookshelf in the back.

As she walked away, he again let his eyes wander over her legs.

She was as easy on the eyes as a summer sunset. But he knew he needed to be more careful—if he got caught staring by the wrong Jane, he'd be out on the street.

❖

Marigold was the proprietor of Hardboiled, a bookshop that specialized in detective fiction. He got enough foot traffic to keep the doors open, but he knew he needed to be in a nicer location if he really wanted to bring in some cheddar. Hardboiled was a dive on Chicago's South Side, and it looked like a place you'd go if you wanted to be relieved of your wallet.

Among the needed improvements was a more prominent sign. Marigold liked to tell potential patrons that they practically had to be a detective to find the shop.

It was a joke he'd been telling for twenty-five years. It had aged well, unlike the man himself. He was just north of fifty years old, but he could be mistaken for sixty-five. He had a horseshoe hairline with unruly tufts poking out the sides, a painfully large belly, and a red, pockmarked face. He looked like the goon squad had worked him over.

His shop wasn't a beauty either. But there was one thing Marigold loved about it—the frosted-glass windows in the front doors. They made it look like an old-timey detective office. Marigold was proud of those windows and cleaned them every morning before opening.

"All set."

It was the cheese-melting lady, come to pay. He rang up her book, gave her a smile, and told her to tell her friends about the store.

As she walked out the door, she swiveled her hips in a manner that would put a lesser man in a coma.

She cast a glance back and caught him staring at her again. She furrowed her brows and said, "Pervert."

He turned red and looked down. His habit of narrating—and staring while doing it—was one he just couldn't break. It had gotten worse as he aged. He supposed it was because he was lonely and bored. After so many years, he had read every book in the store. Twice. And the clientele no longer surprised him. Not even when they came in to ask about eggs. Yeah, eggs. It was always the same thing:

"Excuse me, where are the eggs?" the poor rube would ask. Experience taught Marigold that it wasn't the food section they were after.

"This is a bookstore. We specialize in detective fiction, hence the name of the store." Here he gestured to the front and received a blank stare in return. "Hardboiled detective stories. Like Bogart?" This time he gestured to the posters that adorned one wall. They were of Bogie in his Sam Spade and Philip Marlowe roles.

Frequently the customer still wore a blank stare and Marigold would have to get a bit rude.

"Have you ever seen a store that sells only eggs? And not only that, only a very particular type of egg?"

About ten years ago, he added a small sign atop the doors out front that read "Selling detective fiction since 1996." It had cut such incidents back ever so slightly.

What Marigold dreamed of was being a detective himself. From his years of reading mysteries, he figured he knew just about everything there was to know about crime-solving. And surely any case, even the most mundane, was more exciting and romantic than sitting behind a cash register all day. Sure, he loved his bookstore, but there was little excitement, and it was too restricting. He wanted to call a dish a dish, a dope a dope. He wanted to crack wise and not give a damn. He wanted to be Marlowe.

But he was just an aging man who had too little money, too many bills, and about as many romantic prospects as a grifter has scruples.

Marigold was looking for a copy of "The Murder of Roger Ackroyd" that his computer assured him he had in stock when there was a knock at the front door. He looked up, confused. The door was unlocked, and the store hours were clearly printed beside the windows. He continued searching, certain the knock had been a mistake. Then it came again. Marigold spotted the book he wanted and snatched it off the shelf before he headed to the door.

He opened it to reveal a nervous-looking man. *He was sweaty and thin, so thin he could slip through the crack of a door. He was well-dressed, but the clothes a size too big, and as wrinkled as an elephant's backside.*

"May I help you?" Marigold said.

"Uh, hi. Is this Hardboiled?"

"Yes. We don't sell eggs, if that's what you're inquiring about."

"No, no. I, um, am looking for someone to ... that is, uh, I'm interested in hiring a private, um, investigator. Are you him?"

"That's a new one, Mac," Marigold said.

"Huh?"

"I'm sorry, you've misunderstood. This is a bookstore. The closest thing we have to a detective is Hercule Poirot here," he said, holding up the book he had found.

"Oh," the man said and walked away.

Marigold shook his head in disbelief. A private eye's office. Ridiculous.

He walked back to the counter but stopped in his tracks before he reached it. Wait a sec. *Was* it ridiculous? This is what he dreamed about happening!

Marigold hurried back to the front of the shop and flung open the door. He looked both ways down the street but didn't see the man. He cursed and closed the door despondently.

Destiny had come calling, and he had shut the door in its face. He was a pathetic excuse for a man. His ma sure knew what she was doing when she named him Emery Marigold.

Marigold sat at his desk. He was supposed to be filling orders, but he couldn't stop thinking about the morning's events. Why couldn't he say he was a PI and take a small case? If it went well, he could look into getting a license. The coppers wouldn't give him grief just for one small case. Besides, he could say he was only doing a personal favor.

He pulled out a fake cigarette from his top drawer and pretended to puff on it while he put his feet up.

"That's right, fella, I said scram, or you're gonna catch lead from my good friend here," he said aloud and patted a drawer. He pulled out a water pistol and aimed it at a book. "Kapow."

The phone rang, startling him. He dropped the pistol, and the cheap plastic shattered on the hard wooden floor. He frowned and answered the phone.

"Hardboiled. What can I do for you?"

"Um, hi, I was wondering if, um, you could give me the name of a PI. Uh, I'm, I have a case."

"You the mug who was here this morning?" Marigold asked.

"Mug?"

"Guy. Were you here this morning?"

"Yeah, I um." He didn't finish the sentence.

"I decided I'll take the case." And then he said the line he had rehearsed multiple times a day for the past decade. "The name's Codger," he snarled. "Codger Wolfram. You can call me Ol' Codger. I'm cranky, but I get the job done neat and fast. Whaddya got?"

"Oh, you'll take it? Thank you! I don't know any detectives, and I thought ... yeah."

"What's the case, pal?"

"Um, I'd rather not discuss it over the phone. Can you, uh, meet me later? I could ... no, how about the bar near your store? At five?"

"I'd have to close early, but I'll tell you what—you send enough scratch my way, and you've got me at five."

"Huh?"

"Just make it worth my time. I'll see you then."

Marigold checked the time. Four o'clock already. Well, all he needed to do was fill a couple of orders and drop them in the mail, and he'd be done for the day. He could close up early—it was a slow day for foot traffic anyway.

As he prepared to depart, Marigold opened the janitor's closet. Hanging from the rod was a tan trenchcoat, and on a side hook was a fedora. He had gotten both from a Halloween shop. They looked as genuine as a three-dollar bill.

He stared at them for a bit, embarrassed to wear them yet really wanting to. After a moment, he grabbed the fedora but left the trenchcoat. He went to the bathroom to look himself over.

He adjusted his hat and glowered into the mirror. *The fedora sat at a jaunty angle. It said, It's business time, and you better recognize or get out of the way, or you'll be staring down the wrong end of my bean-shooter.*

The bell tinkled as he left. He locked up and, as was his routine, checked the handle twice. He thought this obsessive little behavior would serve him well as a PI.

He walked into the bar at four-fifty—he wanted to be early for his first case. He took a seat at a corner table, his back to the wall.

"Can I get you something to drink?" a chipper waitress asked. She was no stranger to unconventional customers, but she couldn't help but scrutinize Marigold's fedora, as if unsure if it was a hat or a dead animal sitting on his head. She wore a wary smile as he placed his order.

"I'll take a double scotch. Then come back in about ten minutes, Blondie. I have company coming."

"Ohhhkay," she replied and walked away. She'd never been called Blondie and wasn't sure how she felt about it. Somebody needed to keep an eye on this screwball, she thought.

At five sharp, the nervous man walked in, and Marigold waved to get his attention. *Nervous Man walked quickly, his head down as if he could make the world go away if he didn't look. The man approached a seat and jumped into it like the floor was made of lava.*

"My, uh, case has to do with my, um, wife," he said.

"Whoa, slow down, fella. Why don't we order some drinks. I don't even know your name."

"I'll take a, uh, gin," he said, as if Marigold was the waiter.

Marigold called the waitress over and ordered the gin and another double scotch for himself. After they'd both taken a swallow, Marigold directed Nervous Man to begin.

"My wife, she .. oh, yeah, my name. I'm Milo. My wife is, that is, I suspect she's, um, cheating on me." He lowered his voice and whispered the last part as if he was sharing top-secret information. "I want you to, uh, 'trail' her. Is that the word?"

"Tail. But yeah, I can do that. Do you have a photo of her?" Marigold tossed back the glass and finished his drink. He was really feeling it. He wasn't much of a drinker. In fact, he averaged about one drink a year, on his birthday. The hooch was hitting fast and hard.

Milo showed him a photo and provided a few more details. He laid out the plan. "The easiest thing, um, is if you 'tail' her after she leaves work at, uh, six. See who she's with and if she ... well, you know. I, yeah."

"When I'm tailing someone like that, my fee is a c-note an hour. You good for that?"

Milo stared at him blankly.

"A hundred."

"Okay."

Milo gave him a few more details, and that was that. Detective Wolfram's first case.

He stood up to leave and almost fell over.

"That's some damn fine scotch," he told a random woman on his way out.

Marigold took a hack downtown and waited outside the building he had been directed to. Just after six, he saw Milo's wife. He double-checked the print Milo gave him. Yeah, that's gotta be her, he thought, and started to follow her.

He couldn't walk straight because of the scotch and was about as conspicuous as a peacock in a snowstorm. Even though the streets were crowded, people gave him a wide berth.

He tried to keep his eyes on the broad but couldn't focus, and he soon got confused about which one he was tailing. He checked his notebook. He had only written down "Milo's wife." Not too helpful, you sap, he chided himself.

He kept on following the woman, though, and soon she turned into an alley and got into the passenger seat of a sports car. The driver started to pull away, and Marigold, fearful he would lose her so quickly on his first case, hurried to the car and practically fell onto the hood. He banged it with one fist and yelled, "Hey!"

The driver's side window rolled down, and an angry man in sunglasses yelled at him.

"Get the hell off my car!"

"No, hold on, I need to talk to the skirt," he slurred.

"What'd you call her?"

"Nothing, I just need —"

"You need to back the hell off NOW."

Marigold staggered back, but as the car started moving again, he banged the side in frustration. He had blown his first case.

The brake lights came on, and he knew he should probably leave. But he was sauced and naive, a losing combination. *Mr. Sunglasses didn't seem like someone you'd meet at a church picnic, but the gumshoe thought he had seen a kindness in his face that said, "Hey, I might be tough, but I have a soft spot for puppies."*

The driver leaned out his window, and a gun followed. He pointed it at Marigold and fired once, then sped off.

Marigold felt a pain in his chest and rubbed the area reflexively. His hand came back bloody, and he stared at it in disbelief for a moment. Then he began narrating aloud as if he was talking about someone else.

"Codger Wolfram realized he'd been plugged by the goon. And on his first case, no less. ... He'd miscalculated. ... Rookie mistake. ... It was something he'd laugh about ... for years ... ."

He stumbled forward and collapsed. His face slammed into the concrete and he was dead in minutes.

So ended the career of Detective Wolfram.

RACHEL

BY DEBRA DAUGHERTY

A HIGH SCHOOL built on top of an old cemetery is rumored to be haunted by a young girl named Rachel. Would you attend? Numerous students in Springfield, Illinois have no choice.

Many Springfield High School students believe Rachel roams the halls of their school. She plays tricks with the elevator leading to the boiler room, and the library, auditorium, book repository, art room, and music room are considered *hot spots* for Rachel, as well as other ghostly visitors. But why are they here?

In 1843, cabinetmaker and undertaker, John Hutchinson, established the first private burial ground in the city of Springfield, Hutchinson Cemetery. As a carpenter, he built many of the pine coffins used to inter the residents. Over the years, this cemetery received over seven hundred remains, including the fourth governor of Illinois and United States Senator, William L. D. Ewing, and Abraham and Mary Todd Lincoln's three-year-old son, Edward '*Eddie*', who died in 1850.

On May 14, 1856, the Springfield City Council passed an ordinance that outlawed burials within the city limits. Over six hundred bodies were eventually exhumed from Hutchinson Cemetery and moved to Oak Ridge Cemetery, north of the city. However, as many as one hundred and fifty poor souls were left behind. Some were too decayed. Several could not be found, and many families couldn't afford to reinter their loved ones.

Years passed. City workers planted trees on top of the old cemetery, and it blossomed into a beautiful city park. The citizens of Springfield enjoyed picnicking and strolling through Forest Park, only a few blocks from the State Capital building.

In 1915, the Springfield School District acquired this once hallowed ground for the city's fourth Springfield High School. The new school opened in 1917. Rachel didn't appear until much later.

During renovations on the school in 1983, a construction crew, while digging a shaft for an elevator to the boiler room, struck a grave marker.

The marker offered no name, just the words '*OUR DAUGHTER*' carved across the top, and the inscription, '*CUT DOWN BUT NOT DESTROYED*' chiseled on the front side. The workers placed this grave-stone on a cart in the boiler room. A newspaper photographer reportedly dropped the stone, and a bottom corner section broke off.

Not long after this tombstone was discovered, paranormal activities began to occur. The door of the elevator leading to the boiler room opened without anyone pushing the button. The air in *hot spot* rooms suddenly grew cold. Lights flickered. The faucet in the boys' bathroom inexplicably turned on. Books moved from one side of a table to the other, and many students and staff heard voices, and even glimpsed a ghostly child.

This nameless child connected to the tombstone was haunting their school. The students called this young girl '*Rachel*', a moniker bestowed upon her by a custodian. He named her after his granddaughter.

Rachel's legend grew.

One utility worker, who had seen Rachel several times, refused to ride the elevator to the boiler room. He placed his tools on the elevator, took the stairs, and retrieved his tools when the elevator reached his floor.

While repairing the air conditioner at the school, one of the workmen saw a young girl wearing an eyelet dress. "You shouldn't be in this tunnel," he told her.

Without a word, the girl glided down the hallway and around a corner.

The man followed her, but when he turned the corner, she was gone. "Where did that girl go?" he asked his helper.

"What are you talking about?" the man answered. "There's no girl down here."

Several days later, the same worker saw the girl again. He left his bag of tools and dashed out of the school. He refused to return, even for his tools.

Art teacher Cindy Huffman drew Rachel's likeness on a legal pad, based on the description from a custodian who had seen her many times. Her drawing filled two pages. Cindy taped the pages together and tacked Rachel's picture on the wall in the boiler room. A week later, the drawing disappeared. Cindy asked the custodian what he had done with it.

"I thought you took it," he said.

After a thorough search, the drawing was found. The tape had been removed, and the two pages were once again attached to the legal pad. All the perforations were back in place.

In 2009, the Student Film Club produced a documentary on Rachel. They invited the Springfield Ghost Society to their school. The paranormal research investigators arrived with cameras, camcorders, video recorders, EMF meters to measure electromagnetic fields, and a thermal gun. A video taken during this time showed the moment one of the investigators spoke to a spirit who could have been Rachel. Only she could hear the spirit, and she repeated to the other investigators what the child told her.

"Can you tell me how old you are?" she asked.

"I am twelve."

"Can you tell me how you died?"

"You asked me how I died? My pa is really mad. Have you ever had a rope tied to your feet with a big rock?"

The investigator, visibly affected by the young girl's answer, buries her face in her hands and shakes her head.

The ghost had more to say. "There is an area not far from the town that we moved to. Pa got really mad. Kept telling me to be quiet, so I did, and he threw me in the water in the creek. That's all I remember."

"Can you help me? Can you go to that creek and help me get out of that water?" the spirit pleaded.

The Springfield Ghost Society's paranormal investigators believe Rachel's real name is Megan, the name the ghost gave them. The members of this group also met other specters during their time at the school, an elderly gentleman, Wilbur Matheson, and someone called Emily. The investigators left the school, sad and disappointed because they were unable to help the spirit child.

Rachel makes her presence known in several ways. Some students hear voices or footsteps in the hallway. One girl said she felt someone touch her shoulder, while another thought someone was behind her, but in each case, when they turned around, no one was there.

A teacher found herself alone in the book repository. The lights went off, and she experienced a spine-tingling chill, like a cold breeze passing through her. She rushed out of the room in fear.

Not all of the students or staff are afraid of Rachel. Some don't believe the stories, while others make jokes to allay their fears. When the elevator door opens without the button being pushed, and with no one inside, many say, "Thank you, Rachel."

One time, the lights in the auditorium were turned off by unseen hands. A teacher shouted, "Turn on the lights, Rachel," and the lights came on.

A night custodian should have many stories about Rachel to share, but one retired custodian admitted to the students filming the documentary that he had never seen Rachel, but always wished he had.

In the front of the high school stands a black informational marker. Its text gives a brief history of Hutchinson Cemetery, and of the school. Notable graduates, such as the famous American Poet, Vachel Lindsay, and Brigadier General Edward J. McClernand, a Medal of Honor winner, are listed on this plaque.

One ominous phrase about the cemetery stands out. It states, "Eventually, most of the bodies were exhumed and moved to Oak Ridge Cemetery on Springfield's north side."

Most of the bodies. Not all.

May Rachel, and all the others who were left behind, rest in peace.

Actress Myrna Loy, 1941

EDITOR'S NOTE

Bᴙ RITISH Wᴙ RITER A. M. Burrage (Alfred McLelland Burrage) began writing in his teenage years and is best known for his ghost stories. Perhaps in his time he was fairly well-known, but in my opinion he is very underrated and mostly unrecognized today.

In a not too distant future issue we will be giving more pages to A. M. Burrage, and have much more to say about him. At the time of this writing, you can listen to a radio adaptation from BBC Radio (1963) of The Waxwork, also written by Burrage, on our website. For now, enjoy our holiday offering of *Smee*.

SMEE

A.M. BARRAGE

'**N**O,' SAID JACKSON, with a deprecatory smile, 'I'm sorry. I don't want to upset your game. I shan't be doing that because you'll have plenty without me. But I'm not playing any games of hide-and-seek.'

It was Christmas Eve, and we were a party of fourteen with just the proper leavening of youth. We had dined well; it was the season for childish games, and we were all in the mood for playing them—all, that is, except Jackson. When somebody suggested hide-and-seek there was rapturous and almost unanimous approval. His was the one dissentient voice.

It was not like Jackson to spoil sport or refuse to do as others wanted. Somebody asked him if he were feeling seedy.

'No,' he answered, 'I feel perfectly fit, thanks. But,' he added with a smile which softened without retracting the flat refusal, 'I'm not playing hide-and-seek.'

One of us asked him why not. He hesitated for some seconds before replying.

'I sometimes go and stay at a house where a girl was killed through playing hide-and-seek in the dark. She didn't know the house very well. There was a servants' staircase with a door to it. When she was pursued she opened the door and jumped into what she must have thought was one of the bedrooms—and she broke her neck at the bottom of the stairs.'

We all looked concerned, and Mrs Fernley said:

'How awful! And you were there when it happened?'

Jackson shook his head very gravely. 'No,' he said, 'but I was there when something else happened. Something worse.'

'I shouldn't have thought anything could be worse.'

'This was,' said Jackson, and shuddered visibly. 'Or so it seemed to me.'

I think he wanted to tell the story and was angling for encouragement.

A few requests which may have seemed to him to lack urgency, he affected to ignore and went off at a tangent.

'I wonder if any of you have played a game called "Smee". It's a great improvement on the ordinary game of hide-and-seek. The name derives from the ungrammatical colloquialism, "It's me." You might care to play if you're going to play a game of that sort. Let me tell you the rules.

'Every player is presented with a sheet of paper. All the sheets are blank except one, on which is written "Smee". Nobody knows who is "Smee" except "Smee" himself—or herself, as the case may be. The lights are then turned out and "Smee" slips from the room and goes off to hide, and after an interval the other players go off in search, without knowing whom they are actually in search of. One player meeting another challenges with the word "Smee" and the other player, if not the one concerned, answers "Smee".

'The real "Smee" makes no answer when challenged, and the second player remains quietly by him. Presently they will be discovered by a third player, who, having challenged and received no answer, will link up with the first two. This goes on until all the players have formed a chain, and the last to join is marked down for a forfeit. It's a good noisy, romping game, and in a big house it often takes a long time to complete the chain. You might care to try it; and I'll pay my forfeit and smoke one of Tim's excellent cigars here by the fire until you get tired of it.'

I remarked that it sounded a good game and asked Jackson if he had played it himself. 'Yes,' he answered; 'I played it in the house I was telling you about.'

'And *she* was there? The girl who broke—'

'No, no,' Mrs Fernley interrupted. 'He told us he wasn't there when it happened.'

Jackson considered. 'I don't know if she was there or not. I'm afraid she was. I know that there were thirteen of us and there ought only to have been twelve. And I'll swear that I didn't know her name, or I think I should have gone clean off my head when I heard that whisper in the dark. No, you don't catch me playing that game, or any other like it, any more. It spoiled my nerve quite a while, and I can't afford to take long holidays. Besides, it saves a lot of trouble and inconvenience to own up at once to being a coward.'

Tim Vouce, the best of hosts, smiled around at us, and in that smile there was a meaning which is sometimes vulgarly expressed by the slow closing of an eye. 'There's a story coming,' he announced.

'There's certainly a story of sorts,' said Jackson, 'but whether it's coming or not—' He paused and shrugged his shoulders.

'Well, you're going to pay a forfeit instead of playing?'

'Please. But have a heart and let me down lightly. It's not just a sheer cussedness on my part.'

'Payment in advance,' said Tim, 'insures honesty and promotes good feeling. You are therefore sentenced to tell the story here and now.'

And here follows Jackson's story, unrevised by me and passed on without comment to a wider public:

Some of you, I know, have run across the Sangstons. Christopher Sangston and his wife, I mean. They're distant connections of mine— at least, Violet Sangston is. About eight years ago they bought a house between the North and South Downs on the Surrey and Sussex border, and five years ago they invited me to come and spend Christmas with them.

It was a fairly old house—I couldn't say exactly of what period—and it certainly deserved the epithet 'rambling'. It wasn't a particularly big house, but the original architect, whoever he may have been, had not concerned himself with economising in space, and at first you could get lost in it quite easily.

Well, I went down for that Christmas, assured by Violet's letter that I knew most of my fellow-guests and that the two or three who might be strangers to me were all 'lambs'. Unfortunately, I'm one of the world's workers, and couldn't get away until Christmas Eve, although the other members of the party had assembled on the preceding day. Even then I had to cut it rather fine to be there for dinner on my first night. They were all dressing when I arrived and I had to go straight to my room and waste no time. I may even have kept dinner waiting a bit, for I was last down, and it was announced within a minute of my entering the drawing-room. There was just time to say 'hullo' to everybody I knew, to be briefly introduced to the two or three I didn't know, and then I had to give my arm to Mrs Gorman.

I mention this as the reason why I didn't catch the name of a tall, dark, handsome girl I hadn't met before. Everything was rather hurried and I am always bad at catching people's names. She looked cold and clever and rather forbidding, the sort of girl who gives the impression of knowing all about men and the more she knows of them the less she likes them. I felt that I wasn't going to hit it off with this particular 'lamb' of Violet's, but she looked interesting all the same, and I wondered who she was. I didn't ask, because I was pretty sure of hearing somebody address her by name before very long.

Unluckily, though, I was a long way off her at table, and as Mrs Gorman was at the top of her form that night I soon forgot to worry about who she might be. Mrs Gorman is one of the most amusing women I know, an outrageous but quite innocent flirt, with a very sprightly wit which isn't always unkind. She can think half a dozen moves ahead in conversation just as an expert can in a game of chess. We were soon sparring, or, rather, I was 'covering' against the ropes, and I quite forgot to ask her in an undertone the name of the cold, proud beauty. The lady on the other side of me was a stranger, or had been until a few minutes since, and I didn't think of seeking information in that quarter.

There was a round dozen of us, including the Sangstons themselves, and we were all young or trying to be. The Sangstons themselves were the oldest members of the party and their son Reggie, in his last year at Marlborough, must have been the youngest. When there was talk of playing games after dinner it was he who suggested 'Smee'. He told us how to play it just as I've described it to you.

His father chipped in as soon as we all understood what was going to be required of us. 'If there are any games of that sort going on in the house,' he said, 'for goodness' sake be careful of the back stairs on the first-floor landing. There's a door to them and I've often meant to take it down. In the dark anybody who doesn't know the house very well might think they were walking into a room. A girl actually did break her neck on those stairs about ten years ago when the Ainsties lived here.'

I asked how it happened.

'Oh,' said Sangston, 'there was a party here one Christmas time and they were playing hide-and-seek as you propose doing. This girl was one of the hiders. She heard somebody coming, ran along the passage to get away, and opened the door of what she thought was a bedroom, evidently with the intention of hiding behind it while her pursuer went past. Unfortunately it was the door leading to the back stairs, and that staircase is as straight and almost as steep as the shaft of a pit. She was dead when they picked her up.'

We all promised for our own sakes to be careful. Mrs Gorman said that she was sure nothing could happen to her, since she was insured by three different firms, and her next-of-kin was a brother whose consistent ill-luck was a byword in the family. You see, none of us had known the unfortunate girl, and as the tragedy was ten years old there was no need to pull long faces about it.

Well, we started the game almost immediately after dinner. The men allowed themselves only five minutes before joining the ladies, and then young Reggie Sangston went round and assured himself that the lights were out all over the house except in the servants' quarters and in the drawing-room where we were assembled. We then got busy with twelve sheets of paper which he twisted into pellets and shook up between his hands before passing them round. Eleven of them were blank, and 'Smee' was written on the twelfth. The person drawing the latter was the one who had to hide. I looked and saw that mine was a blank. A moment later out went the electric lights, and in the darkness I heard somebody get up and creep to the door.

After a minute or so somebody gave a signal and we made a rush for the door. I for one hadn't the least idea which of the party was 'Smee'. For five or ten minutes we were all rushing up and down passages and in and out rooms challenging one another and answering, *Smee?—Smee!*

After a bit the alarums and excursions died down, and I guessed that 'Smee' was found. Eventually I found a chain of people all sitting still and holding their breath on some narrow stairs leading up to a row of attics. I hastily joined it, having challenged and been answered with silence, and presently two more stragglers arrived, each racing the other to avoid being last. Sangston was one of them, indeed it was he who was marked down for a forfeit, and after a little while he remarked in an undertone, 'I think we're all here now, aren't we?'

He struck a match, looked up the shaft of the staircase, and began to count. It wasn't hard, although we just about filled the staircase, for we were sitting each a step or two above the next, and all our heads were visible.

'...nine, ten, eleven, twelve—*thirteen*' he concluded, and then laughed. 'Dash it all, that's one too many!'

The match had burned out and he struck another and began to count. He got as far as twelve, and then uttered an exclamation.

'There are thirteen people here!' he exclaimed. 'I haven't counted myself yet.'

'Oh, nonsense!' I laughed. 'You probably began with yourself, and now you want to count yourself twice.'

Out came his son's electric torch, giving a brighter and steadier light and we all began to count. Of course we numbered twelve.

Sangston laughed.

'Well,' he said, 'I could have sworn I counted thirteen twice.'

From halfway up the stairs came Violet Sangston's voice with a little nervous trill in it. 'I thought there was somebody sitting two steps above me. Have you moved up. Captain Ransome?'

Ransome said that he hadn't: he also said that he thought there was somebody sitting between Violet and himself. Just for a moment there was an uncomfortable Something in the air, a little cold ripple which touched us all. For that little moment it seemed to all of us, I think, that something odd and unpleasant had happened and was liable to happen again. Then we laughed at ourselves and at one another and were comfortable once more. There *were* only twelve of us, and there *could* only have been twelve of us, and there was no argument about it. Still laughing we trooped back to the drawing-room to begin again.

This time I was 'Smee', and Violet Sangston ran me to earth while I was still looking for a hiding-place. That round didn't last long, and we were a chain of twelve within two or three minutes. Afterwards there was a short interval. Violet wanted a wrap fetched for her, and her husband went up to get it from her room. He was no sooner gone than Reggie pulled me by the sleeve. I saw that he was looking pale and sick.

'Quick!' he whispered, 'while father's out of the way. Take me into the smoke room and give me a brandy or a whisky or something.'

Outside the room I asked him what was the matter, but he didn't answer at first, and I thought it better to dose him first and question him afterward. So I mixed him a pretty dark-complexioned brandy and soda which he drank at a gulp and then began to puff as if he had been running.

'I've had rather a turn,' he said to me with a sheepish grin.

'What's the matter?'

'I don't know. You were "Smee" just now, weren't you? Well, of course I didn't know who "Smee" was, and while mother and the others ran into the west wing and found you, I turned east. There's a deep clothes cupboard in my bedroom — I'd marked it down as a good place to hide when it was my turn, and I had an idea that "Smee" might be there. I opened the door in the dark, felt round, and touched somebody's hand. "Smee?" I whispered, and not getting any answer I thought I had found "Smee".'

'Well, I don't know how it was, but an odd creepy feeling came over me, I can't describe it, but I felt that something was wrong. So I turned on my electric torch and there was nobody there. Now, I swear I touched a hand, and I was filling up the doorway of the cupboard at the time, so nobody could get out and past me.' He puffed again. 'What do you make of it?' he asked.

'You imagined that you had touched a hand,' I answered, naturally enough.

He uttered a short laugh. 'Of course I knew you were going to say that,' he said. 'I must have imagined it, mustn't I?' He paused and swallowed. 'I mean, it couldn't have been anything else *but* imagination, could it?'

I assured him that it couldn't, meaning what I said, and he accepted this, but rather with the philosophy of one who knows he is right but doesn't expect to be believed. We returned together to the drawing-room where, by that time, they were all waiting for us and ready to start again.

It may have been my imagination—although I'm almost sure it wasn't—but it seemed to me that all enthusiasm for the game had suddenly melted like a white frost in strong sunlight. If anybody had suggested another game I'm sure we should all have been grateful and abandoned 'Smee'. Only nobody did. Nobody seemed to like to. I for one, and I can speak for some of the others too, was oppressed with the feeling that there was something wrong. I couldn't have said what I thought was wrong, indeed I didn't think about it at all, but somehow all the sparkle had gone out of the fun, and hovering over my mind like a shadow was the warning of some sixth sense which told me that there was an influence in the house which was neither sane, sound nor healthy. Why did I feel like that? Because Sangston had counted thirteen of us instead of twelve, and his son had thought he had touched somebody in an empty cupboard.

No, there was more in it than just that. One would have laughed at such things in the ordinary way, and it was just that feeling of something being wrong which stopped me from laughing.

Well, we started again, and when we went in pursuit of the unknown 'Smee', we were as noisy as ever, but it seemed to me that most of us were acting. Frankly, for no reason other than the one I've given you, we'd stopped enjoying the game. I had an instinct to hunt with the main pack, but after a few minutes, during which no 'Smee' had been found, my instinct to play winning games and be first if possible, set me searching on my own account. And on the first floor of the west wing following the wall which was actually the shell of the house, I blundered against a pair of human knees.

I put out my hand and touched a soft, heavy curtain. Then I knew where I was. There were tall, deeply-recessed windows with seats along the landing, and curtains over the recesses to the ground. Somebody was sitting in a corner of this window-seat behind the curtain. Aha, I had caught 'Smee'! So I drew the curtain aside, stepped in, and touched the bare arm of a woman.

It was a dark night outside, and, moreover, the window was not only curtained but a blind hung down to where the bottom panes joined up with the frame. Between the curtain and the window it was as dark as the plague of Egypt. I could not have seen my hand held six inches before my face, much less the woman sitting in the corner.

'Smee?' I whispered.

I had no answer. 'Smee' when challenged does not answer. So I sat beside her, first in the field, to await the others. Then, having settled myself I leaned over to her and whispered:

'Who is it? What's your name, "Smee"?'

And out of the darkness beside me the whisper came back: 'Brenda Ford.'

I didn't know the name, but because I didn't know it I guessed at once who she was. The tall, pale, dark girl was the only person in the house I didn't know by name. Ergo my companion was the tall, pale, dark girl. It seemed rather intriguing to be there with her, shut in between a heavy curtain and a window, and I rather wondered whether she was enjoying the game we were all playing. Somehow she hadn't seemed to me to be one of the romping sort. I muttered one or two commonplace questions to her and had no answer.

'Smee' is a game of silence. 'Smee' and the person or persons who have found 'Smee' are supposed to keep quiet to make it hard for the others. But there was nobody else about, and it occurred to me that she was playing the game a little too much to the letter. I spoke again and got no answer, and then I began to be annoyed. She was of that cold, 'superior' type which affects to despise men; she didn't like me; and she was sheltering behind the rules of a game for children to be dis-courteous. Well, if she didn't like sitting there with me, I certainly didn't want to be sitting there with her! I half turned from her and began to hope that we should both be discovered without much more delay.

Having discovered that I didn't like being there alone with her, it was queer how soon I found myself hating it, and that for a reason very different from the one which had at first whetted my annoyance. The girl I had met for the first time before dinner, and seen diagonally across the table, had a sort of cold charm about her which had attracted while it had half angered me. For the girl who was with me, imprisoned in the opaque darkness between the curtain and the window, I felt no attraction at all. It was so very much the reverse that I should have wondered at myself if, after the first shock of the discovery that she had suddenly become repellent to me, I had had room in my mind for anything besides the consciousness that her close presence was an increasing horror to me.

It came upon me just as quickly as I've uttered the words. My flesh suddenly shrank from her as you see a strip of gelatine shrink and wither before the heat of a fire. That feeling of something being wrong had come back to me, but multiplied to an extent which turned foreboding into actual terror. I firmly believe that I should have got up and run if I had not felt that at my first movement she would have divined my intention and compelled me to stay, by some means of which I could not bear to think. The memory of having touched her bare arm made me wince and draw in my lips. I prayed that somebody else would come along soon.

My prayer was answered. Light footfalls sounded on the landing. Somebody on the other side of the curtain brushed again my knees. The curtain was drawn aside and a woman's hand, fumbling in the darkness, presently rested on my shoulder. 'Smee?' whispered a voice which I instantly recognised as Mrs Gorman's.

Of course she received no answer. She came and settled down beside me with a rustle, and I can't describe the sense of relief she brought me.

'It's Tony, isn't it?' she whispered.

'Yes,' I whispered back.

'You're not "Smee" are you?'

'No, she's on my other side.'

She reached a hand across me, and I heard one of her nails scratch the surface of a woman's silk gown.

'Hullo, "Smee"! How are you? Who are you? Oh, is it against the rules to talk? Never mind, Tony, we'll break the rules. Do you know, Tony, this game is beginning to irk me a little. I hope they're not going to run it to death by playing it all the evening. I'd like to play some game where we can all be together in the same room with a nice bright fire.'

'Same here,' I agreed fervently.

'Can't you suggest something when we go down? There's something rather uncanny in this particular amusement. I can't quite shed the delusion that there's somebody in this game who oughtn't to be in at all.'

That was just how I had been feeling, but I didn't say so. But for my part the worst of my qualms were now gone; the arrival of Mrs Gorman had dissipated them. We sat on talking, wondering from time to time when the rest of the party would arrive.

I don't know how long elapsed before we heard a clatter of feet on the landing and young Reggie's voice shouting, 'Hullo! Hullo, there! Anybody there?'

'Yes,' I answered.

'Mrs Gorman with you?'

'Yes.'

'Well, you're a nice pair! You've both forfeited. We've all been waiting you for hours.'

'Why, you haven't found "Smee" yet,' I objected.

'*You* haven't, you mean. I happen to have been "Smee" myself.'

'But "Smee's" here with us,' I cried.

'Yes,' agreed Mrs Gorman.

The curtain was stripped aside and in a moment we were blinking into the eye of Reggie's electric torch. I looked at Mrs Gorman and then on my other side. Between me and the wall there was an empty space on the window seat. I stood up at once and wished I hadn't, for I found myself sick and dizzy.

'There was somebody there,' I maintained, 'because I touched her.'

'So did I,' said Mrs Gorman in a voice which had lost its steadiness. 'And I don't see how she could have got up and gone without our knowing it.'

Reggie uttered a queer, shaken laugh. He, too, had had an unpleasant experience that evening. 'Somebody's been playing the goat,' he remarked. 'Coming down?'

We were not very popular when we arrived in the drawing-room. Reggie rather tactlessly gave it out that he had found us sitting on a window-seat behind the curtain. I taxed the tall, dark girl with having pretended to be 'Smee' and afterwards slipping away. She denied it. After which we settled down and played other games. 'Smee' was done with for the evening, and I for one was glad of it.

Some long while later, during an interval, Sangston told me, if I wanted a drink, to go into the smoke room and help myself. I went, and he presently followed me. I could see that he was rather peeved with me, and the reason came out during the following minute or two. It seemed that, in his opinion, if I must sit out and flirt with Mrs Gorman—in circumstances which would have been considered highly compromising in his young days—I needn't do it during a round game and keep everybody waiting for us.

'But there was somebody else there,' I protested, 'somebody pretending to be "Smee". I believe it was that tall, dark girl. Miss Ford, although she denied it. She even whispered her name to me.'

Sangston stared at me and nearly dropped his glass.

'Miss *Who?*' he shouted.

'Brenda Ford—she told me her name was.'

Sangston put down his glass and laid a hand on my shoulder.

'Look here, old man,' he said, 'I don't mind a joke, but don't let it go too far. We don't want all the women in the house getting hysterical. Brenda Ford is the name of the girl who broke her neck on the stairs playing hide-and-seek here ten years ago.'

End.

MERRY CHRISTMAS AND HAPPY HOLIDAYS TO ALL!

LOOK FOR ISSUE #3 IN SPRING 2022...
AND THANK YOU FOR JOINING IN THE ADVENTURES!

SOURCES

KATHERINE WRIGHT/WRIGHT BROTHERS/ BICYCLE SHOP:

AP Article on Wright Brothers Bicycle Shop:
https://apnews.com/article/ohio-dayton-711a0ffbd040fb918bb254a436003c1e

IMAGES:

Billie Holiday:

Gottlieb, William P. *Portrait of Billie Holiday, Downbeat, New York, N.Y., ca. Feb.*, Monographic. Photograph. Retrieved from the Library of Congress, www.loc.gov/item/gottlieb.04251/.

Japanese Americans:

Lee, Russell, photographer. *Nyssa, Oregon. Japanese-American farm workers have an ice cream soda on weekly trip to town.* July. Photograph. Retrieved from the Library of Congress, http://www.loc.gov/item/2017819414/.

RACHEL:

News Break—Ultimate Unexplained Eric Myer/published October 26, 2020
https://www.newsbreak.com/illinois/springfield/news/2089771518773/springfield-illinois-high-school-was-built-on-cemetery-and-haunted-by-the-ghost-of-rachel

https://ultimateunexplained.com/springfield-illinois-high-school-was-built-on-cemetery-and-haunted-by-the-ghost-of-rachel/

Debbie Lowery—member of the Springfield Ghost Society.
debbie.lowery@comcast.net
Correspondence by email.
http://springfieldghostsociety.com/

Illinois Historical Markers on Waymarking.com
https://www.waymarking.com/waymarks/WM8X5E_Hutchinson_Cemetery_and_Springfield_High_School_Springfield_Illinois

Brody/Johnson YouTube Documentary filmed October, 2009
https://www.bing.com/videos/
search?q=rachel+video+by+spfld+high+school+students%2c+spfld%2c+il&&view=detail&
mid=D5D38BD1C64EB25A4254D5D38BD1C64EB25A4254&&FORM=VRDGAR&
ru=%2Fvideos%2Fsearch%3Fq%3Drachel%2Bvideo%2Bby%2Bspfld%2Bhigh%2Bschool%2Bstudents%252c%2Bspfld%252c%2Bil%26qpvt%3Drachel%2Bvideo%2Bby%2Bspfld%2Bhigh%2Bschool%2Bstudents%252c%2Bspfld%252c%2Bil%26FORM%3DVDRE

Political Graveyard.com Springfield Hutchinson Cemetery Cemeteries and Memorial Sites of Politicians in Sangamon County
http://politicalgraveyard.com/geo/IL/SG-buried.html

Wikipedia Springfield High School Illinois
https://en.wikipedia.org/wiki/Springfield_High_School_(Illinois)

Hutchinson Cemetery
https://www.findagrave.com/cemetery/2098820/hutchinson-cemetery-(defunct)

Oak Ridge Cemetery
https://publish.illinois.edu/ihlc-blog/2019/10/31/oak-ridge-cemetery/

Find a Grave Edward Lincoln
https://www.findagrave.com/memorial/9125/edward-baker-lincoln

Memories of Springfield—Private Facebook Group—(water turned on in boys' bathroom)

October/2020 comments about hauntings in the Springfield, Illinois area. Rachel was discussed.

Timeline:

Hutchinson Cemetery 1843-1874.

Edward "Eddie" Lincoln died February 1, 1850. Buried at Hutchinson Cemetery. Moved to Oak Ridge Cemetery in 1865.

Oak Ridge Cemetery opened 1855. Dedicated May 24, 1860.

Springfield City Council passed an ordinance that outlawed burials within the city limits in 1856.

Springfield decided to build a high school on top of Hutchinson Cemetery in 1915.

Springfield High School opened in 1917.

Rachel's grave marker was dug up in 1983.

The Springfield High School Student Film Club produced a documentary on Rachel in 2009.

Text of informational marker at Springfield High School
Hutchinson Cemetery & Springfield High School:

On this site in 1843, John Hutchinson, undertaker, cabinetmaker, and businessman established the first private burial ground in Springfield, located on the western edge of the then-newly-incorporated city. Hutchinson Cemetery operated for several decades and received the remains of more than 700 of Springfield's earliest and most respected citizens, including land developer Pascal P. Enos, Rev. Charles Dresser, and early Springfield merchant Robert Irwin. Edward Barker "Eddie" Lincoln, the three year old son of Abraham and Mary Lincoln, was buried here in February 1850, as were many other Springfield children who succumbed to infections and diseases no longer considered life-threatening by modern medical standards. The cemetery continued to receive burials through the Civil War, but in 1874, a city ordinance closed Hutchinson. Eventually most of the bodies were exhumed and removed to Oak Ridge Cemetery on Springfield's north side.

The Springfield School District acquired the former cemetery and constructed the present and fourth Springfield High School here in 1917. Built in the Beaux Arts style, the school was considered at the time the most modern public educational faculty in the state. Most of the original exterior architectural details and mosaics remain intact. Notable graduates include: Poet Vachel Lindsay; Homer translator Robert Fitzgerald; educator Susan Wilcox; scientist and presidential advisor Dr. J. Lee Westrate; World Bank director E. Patrick Coady; and Medal of Honor winner, Brigadier General Edward J. McClernand.